THIS BOOK
BELONGS TO:

ABBEY

CHRISTMAS 1992
FROM THE
WHITEMANS

the Sleeping Beauty

AND OTHER CLASSIC FRENCH FAIRY TALES

CHILDREN'S CLASSICS

This unique series of Children's Classics ™ features accessible and highly readable texts paired with the work of talented and brilliant illustrators of bygone days to create fine editions for today's parents and children to rediscover and treasure. Besides being a handsome addition to any home library, this series features genuine bonded-leather spines stamped in gold, full-color illustrations, and high-quality acid-free paper that will enable these books to be passed from one generation to the next.

the Sleeping Beauty

AND OTHER CLASSIC FRENCH FAIRY TALES

Charles Perrault and Madame D'Aulnoy

Illustrated in color by Edmund Dulac, Gustav Tenggren,
and William Heath Robinson

CHILDREN'S CLASSICS
NEW YORK

Originally published under the title *Old-Time Stories,* in a slightly different form.

Foreword and compilation copyright © 1991 by dilithium Press, Ltd.
All rights reserved.

This 1991 edition is published by Children's Classics, a division of dilithium Press, Ltd., distributed by Outlet Book Company, Inc., a Random House Company, 225 Park Avenue South, New York, New York 10003.

DILITHIUM is a registered trademark and CHILDREN'S CLASSICS is a trademark of dilithium Press, Ltd.

Printed and bound in the United States of America

Library of Congress Cataloging-in-Publication Data

Perrault, Charles, 1628–1703.
   [Old-time stories]
   The sleeping beauty and other classic French fairy tales/retold by Charles Perrault and Madame d'Aulnoy; illustrated in color by Edmund Dulac, Gustav Tenggren, and William Heath Robinson.
   p.   cm.
   Originally published: Old-time stories. London: Constable.
   Summary: A collection of twelve classic French fairy tales, including "The Sleeping Beauty in the Wood," "Puss in Boots," and "Blue Beard."
   ISBN 0-517-03706-8: $10.99
   1. Fairy tales—France. [1. Fairy tales. 2. Folklore—France.] I. Aulnoy, Madame d' (Marie-Catherine), 1650 or 51-1705. II. Dulac, Edmund, 1882–1953, ill. III. Tenggren, Gustav, 1896– ill. IV. Robinson, W. Heath (William Heath), 1872–1944, ill. V. Title.
PZ8.P426Sn 1991
[398.2]—dc20   91-3177
                                           CIP
                                         AC

For this edition of The Sleeping Beauty and Other Classic French Fairy Tales:

Cover design: Melissa Ring
Interior design: Don Bender
Production supervision: Susan Wein

Front cover illustration for "The Sleeping Beauty" by Edmund Dulac
Back cover illustration for "Blue Beard" by William Heath Robinson

8   7   6   5   4   3   2   1

CONTENTS

Notes on the Text

The editors advise that parents, aware that fairy tales traditionally have included a certain measure of violence, review these stories before reading them to young children, selecting those best suited to their years and understanding.

In addition, the editors note that many of the stories in this book were originally published in the early twentieth century, and the modern reader may be surprised to discover old-fashioned styles of punctuation and spelling. The text from the original volume used for this Children's Classics edition has been completely reset, but the earlier styles have been retained to convey the flavor of the original work.

Claire Booss
SERIES EDITOR

ILLUSTRATIONS IN COLOR

vii

FOREWORD

THIS delightful collection of old French fairy tales includes the original version of "Sleeping Beauty," along with eleven other stories guaranteed to enchant a young audience. Eight of these classic tales, all originally published in French, are by Charles Perrault (1828–1703); three were written by Marie-Catherine le Jumel de Barneville de la Motte, Comtesse d'Aulnoy (1650–1705), also known as Madame d'Aulnoy. "Beauty and the Beast" comes from the pen of Madame Leprince de Beaumont (1711–1781), who is credited with the first publication of this charming story.

To anyone familiar with the versions of these stories as they were presented by the Brothers Grimm and then further adapted and simplified (throughout several hundred years and even more editions), this collection will have a very different flavor.

Charles Perrault is best known for his work *Tales of Mother Goose; or Stories of Olden Times,* published in 1697 as *Contes de ma*

Foreword

mère l'Oye, which included the first published versions of four strikingly original stories: "The Sleeping Beauty in the Wood," "Cinderella," "Puss in Boots," and "Little Red Riding Hood." "Little Tom Thumb," "The Fairies," "Ricky of the Tuft," and "Blue Beard," also from Perrault's *Tales of Mother Goose,* were derived from sources in oral folklore and previously published popular works. As told in the original Perrault tale, "Sleeping Beauty" has a very different ending than the version which the Brothers Grimm adopted—for they omitted the evil ogre-queen, mother of Prince Charming.

Madame d'Aulnoy, a contemporary of Perrault's, was an extremely inventive if somewhat less dramatic teller of tales. "The Friendly Frog," "Princess Rosette," and "The Yellow Dwarf" all display the complex plots and "court style" that identifies them as d'Aulnoy's. Bits of social satire—frog courtiers huffily denying their reputation as the scum of the marshes, for instance—further enliven these stories, which were originally written for adults as well as children.

Perrault's and d'Aulnoy's stories are very French—the emphasis on food as a device for turning the plot is particularly noteworthy. In "Sleeping Beauty," when the ogre-queen's chief steward is asked to prepare a piquant sauce to enhance the flavor of the rather special meat he has been ordered to serve for dinner, his sauce is so fine that she requests it again, under similar circumstances and with dramatic results. Now a piquant sauce, as any Frenchman would know, is a dark, spicy concoction made with beef stock, pepper, tomatoes, and capers—a sauce that will readily disguise almost any kind of meat. The English, however, unsure of their audience's familiarity with French cuisine, gave a recipe for piquant sauce in

Foreword

the first translated version of Perrault's story. Other gastronomic oddities which will, perhaps, endear themselves more to children than adults include a fly-pastry ("I have a liking for fly-pastries," said the Lion-Witch; "and you must contrive to catch flies enough to make me a large and tasty one"), and a Princess pie requested (but ultimately not eaten) by a dragon ("The dragon, [the giant] said, was so obstinate, and so addicted to the pleasures of the table, that no power on earth would restrain him from eating what he had a mind to make a meal of"). From the moment when even the pheasants roasting on the fire slumber along with Sleeping Beauty, food—its presence, absence, type, and preparation—is an integral part of the plot structure in these very French fairy tales.

This Children's Classics volume also brings together the work of three illustrators: Edmund Dulac, Gustav Tenggren, and William Heath Robinson.

Edmund Dulac (1882–1953) was a French-born artist who became a British subject and was well-known for his imaginative, lyrical book illustrations. Charming examples of his art in this volume are the interior color plates depicting scenes from "Cinderella" and "Blue Beard."

Gustav Tenggren (1896–1970) illustrated numerous children's books in Scandinavia and the United States. His "Yellow Dwarf" appears here among the color plates.

William Heath Robinson (1872–1944), a British artist, was born into a family of book illustrators and engravers. Highly original, witty, and versatile, his work encompassed diverse topics and illustrated the works of authors from Shakespeare to Rabelais and de la Mare. Robinson's black-and-white drawings may be found

Foreword

throughout the book; his color illustrations in the interior plates present "Sleeping Beauty," "Puss in Boots," "Beauty and the Beast," "The Friendly Frog," and "Tom Thumb." Robinson's compositions are quite different from Dulac's atmospheric renditions, but no less effective.

Now that the stage is set and the appetite awakened, let the stories begin.

LOIS HILL

New York
1991

THE SLEEPING BEAUTY
IN THE WOOD

ONCE upon a time there lived a king and queen who were grieved, more grieved than words can tell, because they had no children. They tried the waters of every country, made vows and pilgrimages, and did everything that could be done, but without result. At last, however, the queen found that her wishes were fulfilled, and in due course she gave birth to a daughter.

A grand christening was held, and all the fairies that could be found in the realm (they numbered seven in all) were invited to be godmothers to the little princess. This was done so that by means of the gifts which each in turn would bestow upon her (in accordance with the fairy custom of those days) the princess might be endowed with every imaginable perfection.

When the christening ceremony was over, all the company returned to the king's palace, where a great banquet was held in honour of the fairies. Places were laid for them in magnificent style, and before each was placed a solid gold casket containing a spoon, fork, and knife of fine gold, set with diamonds and rubies. But just as all were sitting down to table an aged fairy was seen to enter, whom no one had thought to invite—the reason being that for more than fifty years she had never quitted the tower in which she lived, and people had supposed her to be dead or bewitched.

Sleeping Beauty

By the king's orders a place was laid for her, but it was impossible to give her a golden casket like the others, for only seven had been made for the seven fairies. The old creature believed that she was intentionally slighted, and muttered threats between her teeth.

She was overheard by one of the young fairies, who was seated near by. The latter, guessing that some mischievous gift might be bestowed upon the little princess, hid behind the tapestry as soon as the company left the table. Her intention was to be the last to speak, and so to have the power of counteracting, as far as possible, any evil which the old fairy might do.

Presently the fairies began to bestow their gifts upon the princess. The youngest ordained that she should be the most beautiful person in the world; the next, that she should have the temper of an angel; the third, that she should do everything with wonderful grace; the fourth, that she should dance to perfection; the fifth, that she should sing like a nightingale; and the sixth, that she should play every kind of music with the utmost skill.

It was now the turn of the aged fairy. Shaking her head, in token of spite rather than of infirmity, she declared that the princess should prick her hand with a spindle, and die of it. A shudder ran through the company at this terrible gift. All eyes were filled with tears.

But at this moment the young fairy stepped forth from behind the tapestry.

"Take comfort, your Majesties," she cried in a loud voice; "your daughter shall not die. My power, it is true, is not enough to undo all that my aged kinswoman has decreed: the princess will indeed prick her hand with a spindle. But instead of dying she shall merely fall into a profound slumber that will last a hundred

The king . . . at once published an edict

years. At the end of that time a king's son shall come to awaken her."

The king, in an attempt to avert the unhappy doom pronounced by the old fairy, at once published an edict forbidding all persons, under pain of death, to use a spinning-wheel or keep a spindle in the house.

At the end of fifteen or sixteen years the king and queen happened one day to be away, on pleasure bent. The princess was running about the castle, and going upstairs from room to room she came at length to a garret at the top of a tower, where an old serving-woman sat alone with her distaff, spinning. This good woman had never heard speak of the king's proclamation forbidding the use of spinning-wheels.

"What are you doing, my good woman?" asked the princess.

"I am spinning, my pretty child," replied the dame, not knowing who she was.

"Oh, what fun!" rejoined the princess; "how do you do it? Let me try and see if I can do it equally well."

Partly because she was too hasty, partly because she was a little heedless, but also because the fairy decree had ordained it, no sooner had she seized the spindle than she pricked her hand and fell down in a swoon.

In great alarm the good dame cried out for help. People came running from every quarter to the princess. They threw water on her face, chafed her with their hands, and rubbed her temples with the royal essence of Hungary. But nothing would restore her.

Then the king, who had been brought upstairs by the commotion, remembered the fairy prophecy. Feeling certain that what had happened was inevitable, since the fairies had decreed it, he gave orders that the princess should be placed in the finest apartment in the palace, upon a bed embroidered in gold and silver.

You would have thought her an angel, so fair was she to behold. The trance had not taken away the lovely colour of her complexion. Her cheeks were delicately flushed, her lips like coral. Her eyes, indeed, were closed, but her gentle breathing could be heard, and it was therefore plain that she was not dead. The king commanded that she should be left to sleep in peace until the hour of her awakening should come.

When the accident happened to the princess, the good fairy who had saved her life by condemning her to sleep a hundred years was in the kingdom of Mataquin, twelve thousand leagues away. She was instantly warned of it, however, by a little dwarf who had a pair of seven-league boots, which are boots that enable one to cover seven leagues at a single step. The fairy set off at once, and within an hour her chariot of fire, drawn by dragons, was seen approaching.

The king handed her down from her chariot, and she approved of all that he had done. But being gifted with great powers of foresight, she bethought herself that when the princess came to be awakened, she would be much distressed to find herself all alone in the old castle. And this is what she did.

She touched with her wand everybody (except the king and queen) who was in the castle—governesses, maids of honour, ladies-in-waiting, gentlemen, officers, stewards, cooks, scullions, errand boys, guards, porters, pages, footmen. She touched likewise all the horses in the stables, with their grooms, the big mastiffs in the courtyard, and little Puff, the pet dog of the princess, who was

A little dwarf who had a pair of seven-league boots

lying on the bed beside his mistress. The moment she had touched them they all fell asleep, to awaken only at the same moment as their mistress. Thus they would always be ready with their service whenever she should require it. The very spits before the fire, loaded with partridges and pheasants, subsided into slumber, and the fire as well. All was done in a moment, for the fairies do not take long over their work.

Then the king and queen kissed their dear child, without waking her, and left the castle. Proclamations were issued, forbidding any approach to it, but these warnings were not needed, for within a quarter of an hour there grew up all round the park so vast a quantity of trees big and small, with interlacing brambles and thorns, that neither man nor beast could penetrate them. The tops alone of the castle towers could be seen, and these only from a distance. Thus did the fairy's magic contrive that the princess, during all the time of her slumber, should have nought whatever to fear from prying eyes.

At the end of a hundred years the throne had passed to another family from that of the sleeping princess. One day the king's son chanced to go a-hunting that way, and seeing in the distance some towers in the midst of a large and dense forest, he asked what they were. His attendants told him in reply the various stories which they had heard. Some said there was an old castle haunted by ghosts, others that all the witches of the neighbourhood held their revels there. The favourite tale was that in the castle lived an ogre, who carried thither all the children whom he could catch. There he dispensed with them at his leisure, and since he was the only person who could force a passage through the wood nobody had been able to pursue him.

Sleeping Beauty

While the prince was wondering what to believe, an old peasant took up the tale.

The king's son chanced to go a-hunting

"Your Highness," said he, "more than fifty years ago I heard my father say that in this castle lies a princess, the most beautiful that has ever been seen. It is her doom to sleep there for a hundred years, and then to be awakened by a king's son, for whose coming she waits."

This story fired the young prince. He jumped immediately to the conclusion that it was for him to see so gay an adventure through, and impelled alike by the wish for love and glory, he resolved to set about it on the spot.

Sleeping Beauty

Hardly had he taken a step towards the wood when the tall trees, the brambles and the thorns, separated of themselves and made a path for him. He turned in the direction of the castle, and espied it at the end of a long avenue. This avenue he entered, and was surprised to notice that the trees closed up again as soon as he had passed, so that none of his retinue were able to follow him. A young and gallant prince is always brave, however; so he continued on his way, and presently reached a large fore-court.

The sight that now met his gaze was enough to fill him with an icy fear. The silence of the place was dreadful, and death seemed all about him. The recumbent figures of men and animals had all the appearance of being lifeless, until he perceived by the pimply noses and ruddy faces of the porters that they merely slept. It was plain, too, from their glasses, in which were still some dregs of wine, that they had fallen asleep while drinking.

The prince made his way into a great courtyard, paved with marble, and mounting the staircase entered the guardroom. Here the guards were lined up on either side in two ranks, their muskets on their shoulders, snoring their hardest. Through several apartments crowded with ladies and gentlemen in waiting, some seated, some standing, but all asleep, he pushed on, and so came at last to a chamber which was decked all over with gold. There he encountered the most beautiful sight he had ever seen. Reclining upon a bed, the curtains of which on every side were drawn back, was a princess of seemingly some fifteen or sixteen summers, whose radiant beauty had an almost unearthly lustre.

Trembling in his admiration he drew near and went on his knees beside her. At the same moment, the hour of disenchantment having come, the princess awoke, and bestowed upon him a look more tender than a first glance might seem to warrant.

All asleep

"Is it you, dear prince?" she said; "you have been long in coming!"

Charmed by these words, and especially by the manner in which they were said, the prince scarcely knew how to express his delight and gratification. He declared that he loved her better than he loved himself. His words were faltering, but they pleased the more for that. The less there is of eloquence, the more there is of love.

Her embarrassment was less than his, and that is not to be wondered at, since she had had time to think of what she would say to him. It seems (although the story says nothing about it) that the good fairy had beguiled her long slumber with pleasant dreams. To be brief, after four hours of talking they had not succeeded in uttering one half of the things they had to say to each other.

Now the whole palace had awakened with the princess. Every one went about his business, and since they were not all in love they presently began to feel mortally hungry. The lady-in-wait-

They all fell asleep

ing, who was suffering like the rest, at length lost patience, and in a loud voice called out to the princess that supper was served.

The princess was already full dressed, and in most magnificent style. As he helped her to rise, the prince refrained from telling her that her clothes, with the straight collar which she wore, were like those to which his grandmother had been accustomed. And in truth, they in no way detracted from her beauty.

They passed into an apartment hung with mirrors, and were there served with supper by the stewards of the household, while the fiddles and oboes played some old music—and played it remarkably well, considering they had not played at all for just upon a hundred years. A little later, when supper was over, the chaplain married them in the castle chapel, and in due course, attended by the courtiers in waiting, they retired to rest.

They slept but little, however. The princess, indeed, had not much need of sleep, and as soon as morning came the prince took his leave of her. He returned to the city, and told his father, who was awaiting him with some anxiety, that he had lost himself while hunting in the forest, but had obtained some black bread and cheese from a charcoalburner, in whose hovel he had passed the night. His royal father, being of an easy-going nature, believed the tale, but his mother was not so easily hoodwinked. She noticed that he now went hunting every day, and that he always had an excuse handy when he had slept two or three nights from home. She felt certain, therefore, that he had some love affair.

Two whole years passed since the marriage of the prince and princess, and during that time they had two children. The first, a daughter, was called "Dawn," while the second, a boy, was named "Day," because he seemed even more beautiful than his sister.

Sleeping Beauty

Many a time the queen told her son that he ought to settle down in life. She tried in this way to make him confide in her, but he did not dare to trust her with his secret. Despite the affection which he bore her, he was afraid of his mother, for she came of a race of ogres, and the king had only married her for her wealth.

It was whispered at the Court that she had ogrish instincts, and that when little children were near her she had the greatest difficulty in the world to keep herself from pouncing on them.

No wonder the prince was reluctant to say a word.

But at the end of two years the king died, and the prince found himself on the throne. He then made public announcement of his marriage, and went in state to fetch his royal consort from her castle. With her two children beside her she made a triumphal entry into the capital of her husband's realm.

Some time afterwards the king declared war on his neighbour, the Emperor Cantalabutte. He appointed the queen-mother as regent in his absence, and entrusted his wife and children to her care.

He expected to be away at the war for the whole of the summer, and as soon as he was gone the queen-mother sent her daughter-in-law and the two children to a country mansion in the forest. This she did that she might be able the more easily to gratify her horrible longings. A few days later she went there herself, and in the evening summoned the chief steward.

"For my dinner to-morrow," she told him, "I will eat little Dawn."

"Oh, Madam!" exclaimed the steward.

"That is my will," said the queen; and she spoke in the tones of an ogre who longs for fresh meat.

"You will serve her with piquant sauce," she added.

Sleeping Beauty

The poor man, seeing plainly that it was useless to trifle with an ogress, took his big knife and went up to little Dawn's chamber. She was at that time four years old, and when she came running with a smile to greet him, flinging her arms round his neck and coaxing him to give her some sweets, he burst into tears, and let the knife fall from his hand.

Presently he went down to the yard behind the house, and slaughtered a young lamb. For this he made so delicious a sauce that his mistress declared she had never eaten anything so good.

At the same time the steward carried little Dawn to his wife, and bade the latter hide her in the quarters which they had below the yard.

Eight days later the wicked queen summoned her steward again.

"For my supper," she announced, "I will eat little Day."

The steward made no answer, being determined to trick her as he had done previously. He went in search of little Day, whom he found with a tiny foil in his hand, making brave passes—though he was but three years old—at a big monkey. He carried him off to his wife, who stowed him away in hiding with little Dawn. To the ogress the steward served up, in place of Day, a young kid so tender that she found it surpassingly delicious.

So far, so good. But there came an evening when this evil queen again addressed the steward.

"I have a mind," she said, "to eat the queen with the same sauce as you served with her children."

This time the poor steward despaired of being able to practise another deception. The young queen was twenty years old, without counting the hundred years she had been asleep. Her skin,

17

though white and beautiful, had become a little tough, and what animal could he possibly find that would correspond to her? He made up his mind that if he would save his own life he must kill the queen, and went upstairs to her apartment determined to do the deed once and for all. Goading himself into a rage he drew his knife and entered the young queen's chamber, but a reluctance to give her no moment of grace made him repeat respectfully the command which he had received from the queen-mother.

"Do it! do it!" she cried, baring her neck to him; "carry out the order you have been given! Then once more I shall see my children, my poor children that I loved so much!"

Nothing had been said to her when the children were stolen away, and she believed them to be dead.

The poor steward was overcome by compassion. "No, no, Madam," he declared; "you shall not die, but you shall certainly see your children again. That will be in my quarters, where I have hidden them. I shall make the queen eat a young hind in place of you, and thus trick her once more."

Without more ado he led her to his quarters, and leaving her there to embrace and weep over her children, proceeded to cook a hind with such art that the queen-mother ate it for her supper with as much appetite as if it had indeed been the young queen.

The queen-mother felt well satisfied with her cruel deeds, and planned to tell the king, on his return, that savage wolves had devoured his consort and his children. It was her habit, however, to prowl often about the courts and alleys of the mansion, in the hope of scenting fresh meat, and one evening she heard the little boy Day crying in a basement cellar. The child was weeping because his mother had threatened to whip him for some naughtiness, and she heard at the same time the voice of Dawn begging forgiveness for her brother.

The ogress recognised the voices of the queen and her children, and was enraged to find she had been tricked. The next morning, in tones so affrighting that all trembled, she ordered a huge vat to be brought into the middle of the courtyard. This she filled with vipers and toads, with snakes and serpents of every kind, intending to cast into it the queen and her children, and the steward with his wife and serving-girl. By her command these were brought forward, with their hands tied behind their backs.

There they were, and her minions were making ready to cast them into the vat, when into the courtyard rode the king! Nobody had expected him so soon, but he had travelled post-haste. Filled with amazement, he demanded to know what this horrible spectacle meant. None dared tell him, and at that moment the ogress, enraged at what confronted her, threw herself head foremost into the vat, and was devoured on the instant by the hideous creatures she had placed in it.

The king could not but be sorry, for after all she was his mother; but it was not long before he found ample consolation in his beautiful wife and children.

The most beautiful sight he had ever seen
Page 11

All that remained for the youngest son was the cat
Page 21

PUSS IN BOOTS

A CERTAIN miller had three sons, and when he died the sole worldly goods which he bequeathed to them were his mill, his ass, and his cat. This little legacy was very quickly divided up, and you may be quite sure that neither notary nor attorney were called in to help, for they would speedily have grabbed it all for themselves.

The eldest son took the mill, and the second son took the ass. Consequently all that remained for the youngest son was the cat, and he was not a little disappointed at receiving such a miserable portion.

"My brothers," said he, "will be able to get a decent living by joining forces, but for my part, as soon as I have eaten my cat and made a muff out of his skin, I am bound to die of hunger."

These remarks were overheard by Puss, who pretended not to have been listening, and said very soberly and seriously:

"There is not the least need for you to worry, Master. All you have to do is to give me a pouch, and get a pair of boots made for me so that I can walk in the woods. You will find then that your share is not so bad after all."

Now this cat had often shown himself capable of performing cunning tricks. When catching rats and mice, for example, he would hide himself amongst the meal and hang downwards by the feet as though he were dead. His master, therefore, though he did not build too much on what the cat had said, felt some hope of being assisted in his miserable plight.

On receiving the boots which he had asked for, Puss gaily pulled them on. Then he hung the pouch round his neck, and holding the cords which tied it in front of him with his paws, he sallied forth to a warren where rabbits abounded. Placing some bran and lettuce in the pouch, he stretched himself out and lay as if dead. His plan was to wait until some young rabbit, unlearned in worldly wisdom, should come and rummage in the pouch for the eatables which he had placed there.

Hardly had he laid himself down when things fell out as he wished. A stupid young rabbit went into the pouch, and Master Puss, pulling the cords tight, killed him on the instant.

Well satisfied with his capture, Puss departed to the king's palace. There he demanded an audience, and was ushered upstairs. He entered the royal apartment, and bowed profoundly to the king.

"I bring you, Sire," said he, "a rabbit from the warren of the marquis of Carabas (such was the title he invented for his master), which I am bidden to present to you on his behalf."

"Tell your master," replied the king, "that I thank him, and am pleased by his attention."

Another time the cat hid himself in a wheatfield, keeping the mouth of his bag wide open. Two partridges ventured in, and by pulling the cords tight he captured both of them. Off he went and presented them to the king, just as he had done with the rabbit from the warren. His Majesty was not less gratified by the brace of partridges, and handed the cat a present for himself.

For two or three months Puss went on in this way, every now

As though he were dead

and again taking to the king, as a present from his master, some game which he had caught. There came a day when he learned that the king intended to take his daughter, who was the most beautiful princess in the world, for an excursion along the river bank.

"If you will do as I tell you," said Puss to his master, "your fortune is made. You have only to go and bathe in the river at the spot which I shall point out to you. Leave the rest to me."

The marquis of Carabas had no idea what plan was afoot, but did as the cat had directed.

While he was bathing the king drew near, and Puss at once began to cry out at the top of his voice:

"Help! help! the marquis of Carabas is drowning!"

At these shouts the king put his head out of the carriage window. He recognised the cat who had so often brought him game, and bade his escort go speedily to the help of the marquis of Carabas.

While they were pulling the poor marquis out of the river, Puss approached the carriage and explained to the king that while his master was bathing robbers had come and taken away his clothes, though he had cried "Stop, thief!" at the top of his voice. As a matter of fact, the rascal had hidden them under a big stone. The king at once commanded the keepers of his wardrobe to go and select a suit of his finest clothes for the marquis of Carabas.

The king received the marquis with many compliments, and as the fine clothes which the latter had just put on set off his good looks (for he was handsome and comely in appearance), the king's daughter found him very much to her liking. Indeed, the marquis of Carabas had not bestowed more than two or three respectful but sentimental glances upon her when she fell madly in love with him. The king invited him to enter the coach and join the party.

W.H.R.

The cat went on ahead

Delighted to see his plan so successfully launched, the cat went on ahead, and presently came upon some peasants who were mowing a field.

"Listen, my good fellows," said he; "if you do not tell the king that the field which you are mowing belongs to the marquis of Carabas, you will all be chopped up into little pieces like mince-meat."

In due course the king asked the mowers to whom the field on which they were at work belonged.

W HEATH ROBINSON

Puss in Boots

Puss in Boots

"It is the property of the marquis of Carabas," they all cried with one voice, for the threat from Puss had frightened them.

"You have inherited a fine estate," the king remarked to Carabas.

"As you see for yourself, Sire," replied the marquis; "this is a meadow which never fails to yield an abundant crop each year."

Still travelling ahead, the cat came upon some harvesters.

"Listen, my good fellows," said he; "if you do not declare that every one of these fields belongs to the marquis of Carabas, you will all be chopped up into little bits like mince-meat."

The king came by a moment later, and wished to know who was the owner of the fields in sight.

"It is the marquis of Carabas," cried the harvesters.

At this the king was more pleased than ever with the marquis.

Preceding the coach on its journey, the cat made the same threat to all whom he met, and the king grew astonished at the great wealth of the marquis of Carabas.

Finally Master Puss reached a splendid castle, which belonged to an ogre. He was the richest ogre that had ever been known, for all the lands through which the king had passed were part of the castle domain.

The cat had taken care to find out who this ogre was, and what powers he possessed. He now asked for an interview, declaring that he was unwilling to pass so close to the castle without having the honour of paying his respects to the owner.

The ogre received him as civilly as an ogre can, and bade him sit down.

"I have been told," said Puss, "that you have the power to

change yourself into any kind of animal—for example, that you can transform yourself into a lion or an elephant."

"That is perfectly true," said the ogre, curtly; "and just to prove it you shall see me turn into a lion."

Puss was so frightened on seeing a lion before him that he sprang on to the roof—not without difficulty and danger, for his boots were not meant for walking on the tiles.

Perceiving presently that the ogre had abandoned his transformation, Puss descended, and owned to having been thoroughly frightened.

"I have also been told," he added, "but I can scarcely believe it, that you have the further power to take the shape of the smallest animals—for example, that you can change yourself into a rat or a mouse. I confess that to me it seems quite impossible."

"Impossible?" cried the ogre; "you shall see!" And in the same moment he changed himself into a mouse, which began to run about the floor. No sooner did Puss see it than he pounced on it and ate it.

Presently the king came along, and noticing the ogre's beautiful mansion desired to visit it. The cat heard the rumble of the coach as it crossed the castle drawbridge, and running out to the courtyard cried to the king:

"Welcome, your Majesty, to the castle of the marquis of Carabas!"

"What's that?" cried the king. "Is this castle also yours, marquis? Nothing could be finer than this courtyard and the buildings which I see all about. With your permission we will go inside and look round."

The marquis gave his hand to the young princess, and fol-

Puss became a personage of great importance

lowed the king as he led the way up the staircase. Entering a great hall they found there a magnificent collation. This had been prepared by the ogre for some friends who were to pay him a visit that very day. The latter had not dared to enter when they learned that the king was there.

The king was now quite as charmed with the excellent qualities of the marquis of Carabas as his daughter. The latter was completely captivated by him. Noting the great wealth of which the marquis was evidently possessed, and having quaffed several cups of wine, he turned to his host, saying:

"It rests with you, marquis, whether you will be my son-in-law."

The marquis, bowing very low, accepted the honour which the king bestowed upon him. The very same day he married the princess.

Puss became a personage of great importance, and gave up hunting mice, except for amusement.

THE FAIRIES

ONCE upon a time there lived a widow with two daughters. The elder was often mistaken for her mother, so like her was she both in nature and in looks; parent and child being so disagreeable and arrogant that no one could live with them.

The younger girl, who took after her father in the gentleness and sweetness of her disposition, was also one of the prettiest girls imaginable. The mother doted on the elder daughter—naturally enough, since she resembled her so closely—and disliked the younger one as intensely. She made the latter live in the kitchen and work hard from morning till night.

One of the poor child's many duties was to go twice a day and draw water from a spring a good half-mile away, bringing it back in a large pitcher. One day when she was at the spring an old woman came up and begged for a drink.

"Why, certainly, good mother," the pretty lass replied. Rinsing her pitcher, she drew some water from the cleanest part of the spring and handed it to the dame, lifting up the jug so that she might drink the more easily.

Now this old woman was a fairy, who had taken the form of a poor village dame to see just how far the girl's good nature would go. "You are so pretty," she said, when she had finished drinking, "and so polite, that I am determined to bestow a gift upon you.

The Fairies

This is the boon I grant you: with every word that you utter there shall fall from your mouth either a flower or a precious stone."

When the girl reached home she was scolded by her mother for being so long in coming back from the spring.

"I am sorry to have been so long, mother," said the poor child.

As she spoke these words there fell from her mouth three roses, three pearls, and three diamonds.

"What's this?" cried her mother; "did I see pearls and diamonds dropping out of your mouth? What does this mean, dear daughter?" (This was the first time she had ever addressed her daughter affectionately.)

The poor child told a simple tale of what had happened, and in speaking scattered diamonds right and left.

"Really," said her mother, "I must send my own child there. Come here, Fanchon; look what comes out of your sister's mouth whenever she speaks! Wouldn't you like to be able to do the same? All you have to do is to go and draw some water at the spring, and when a poor woman asks you for a drink, give it her very nicely."

"Oh, indeed!" replied the ill-mannered girl; "don't you wish you may see me going there!"

"I tell you that you are to go," said her mother, "and to go this instant."

Very sulkily the girl went off, taking with her the best silver flagon in the house. No sooner had she reached the spring than she saw a lady, magnificently attired, who came towards her from the forest, and asked for a drink. This was the same fairy who had appeared to her sister, masquerading now as a princess in order to see how far this girl's ill-nature would carry her.

Lifting up the jug so that she might drink the more easily

The Fairies

"Do you think I have come here just to get you a drink?" said the loutish damsel, arrogantly. "I suppose you think I brought a silver flagon here specially for that purpose—it's so likely, isn't it? Drink from the spring, if you want to!"

"You are not very polite," said the fairy, displaying no sign of anger. "Well, in return for your lack of courtesy I decree that for every word you utter a snake or a toad shall drop out of your mouth."

The moment her mother caught sight of her coming back she cried out, "Well, daughter?"

"Well, mother?" replied the rude girl. As she spoke a viper and a toad were spat out of her mouth.

"Gracious heavens!" cried her mother; "what do I see? Her sister is the cause of this, and I will make her pay for it!"

Off she ran to thrash the poor child, but the latter fled away and hid in the forest near by. The king's son met her on his way home from hunting, and noticing how pretty she was inquired what she was doing all alone, and what she was weeping about.

"Alas, sir," she cried; "my mother has driven me from home!"

As she spoke the prince saw four or five pearls and as many diamonds fall from her mouth. He begged her to tell him how this came about, and she told him the whole story.

The king's son fell in love with her, and reflecting that such a gift as had been bestowed upon her was worth more than any dowry which another maiden might bring him, he took her to the palace of his royal father, and there married her.

As for the sister, she made herself so hateful that even her mother drove her out of the house and nowhere could the wretched girl find any one who would take her in.

RICKY OF THE TUFT

ONCE upon a time there was a queen who bore a son so ugly and misshapen that for some time it was doubtful if he would have human form at all. But a fairy who was present at his birth promised that he should have plenty of brains, and added that by virtue of the gift which she had just bestowed upon him he would be able to impart to the person whom he should love best the same degree of intelligence which he possessed himself.

This somewhat consoled the poor queen, who was greatly disappointed at having brought into the world such a hideous brat. And indeed, no sooner did the child begin to speak than his sayings proved to be full of shrewdness, while all that he did was somehow so clever that he charmed every one.

I forgot to mention that when he was born he had a little tuft of hair upon his head. For this reason he was called Ricky of the Tuft, Ricky being his family name.

Some seven or eight years later the queen of a neighbouring kingdom gave birth to twin daughters. The first one to come into the world was more beautiful than the dawn, and the queen was so overjoyed that it was feared her great excitement might do her some harm. The same fairy who had assisted at the birth of Ricky of the Tuft was present, and, in order to moderate the transports of

41

the queen she declared that this little princess would have no sense at all, and would be as stupid as she was beautiful.

The queen was deeply mortified, and a moment or two later her chagrin became greater still, for the second daughter proved to be extremely ugly.

"Do not be distressed, Madam," said the fairy; "your daughter shall be recompensed in another way. She shall have so much good sense that her lack of beauty will scarcely be noticed."

"May Heaven grant it!" said the queen; "but is there no means by which the elder, who is so beautiful, can be endowed with some intelligence?"

"In the matter of brains I can do nothing for her, Madam," said the fairy, "but as regards beauty I can do a great deal. As there is nothing I would not do to please you, I will bestow upon her the power of making beautiful any person who shall greatly please her."

As the two princesses grew up their perfections increased, and everywhere the beauty of the elder and the wit of the younger were the subject of common talk.

It is equally true that their defects also increased as they became older. The younger grew uglier every minute, and the elder daily became more stupid. Either she answered nothing at all when spoken to, or replied with some idiotic remark. At the same time she was so awkward that she could not set four china vases on the mantelpiece without breaking one of them, nor drink a glass of water without spilling half of it over her clothes.

Now although the elder girl possessed the great advantage which beauty always confers upon youth, she was nevertheless outshone in almost all company by her younger sister. At first

She could not set four china vases on the mantelpiece without breaking one of them

every one gathered round the beauty to see and admire her, but very soon they were all attracted by the graceful and easy conversation of the clever one. In a very short time the elder girl would be left entirely alone, while everybody clustered round her sister.

Graceful and easy conversation

The elder princess was not so stupid that she was not aware of this, and she would willingly have surrendered all her beauty for half her sister's cleverness. Sometimes she was ready to die of grief, for the queen, though a sensible woman, could not refrain from occasionally reproaching her with her stupidity.

Ricky of the Tuft

The princess had retired one day to a wood to bemoan her misfortune, when she saw approaching her an ugly little man, of very disagreeable appearance, but clad in magnificent attire.

This was the young prince Ricky of the Tuft. He had fallen in love with her portrait, which was everywhere to be seen, and had left his father's kingdom in order to have the pleasure of seeing and talking to her.

Delighted to meet her thus alone, he approached with every mark of respect and politeness. But while he paid her the usual compliments he noticed that she was plunged in melancholy.

"I cannot understand, madam," he said, "how any one with your beauty can be so sad as you appear. I can boast of having seen many fair ladies, and I declare that none of them could compare in beauty with you."

"It is very kind of you to say so, sir," answered the princess; and stopped there, at a loss what to say further.

"Beauty," said Ricky, "is of such great advantage that everything else can be disregarded; and I do not see that the possessor of it can have anything much to grieve about."

To this the princess replied:

"I would rather be as plain as you are and have some sense, than be as beautiful as I am and at the same time stupid."

"Nothing more clearly displays good sense, madam, than a belief that one is not possessed of it. It follows, therefore, that the more one has, the more one fears it to be wanting."

"I am not sure about that," said the princess; "but I know only too well that I am very stupid, and this is the reason of the misery which is nearly killing me."

Ricky of the Tuft

"If that is all that troubles you, madam, I can easily put an end to your suffering."

"How will you manage that?" said the princess.

"I am able, madam," said Ricky of the Tuft, "to bestow as much good sense as it is possible to possess on the person whom I love the most. You are that person, and it therefore rests with you to decide whether you will acquire so much intelligence. The only condition is that you shall consent to marry me."

The princess was dumbfounded, and remained silent.

"I can see," pursued Ricky, "that this suggestion perplexes you, and I am not surprised. But I will give you a whole year to make up your mind to it."

The princess had so little sense, and at the same time desired it so ardently, that she persuaded herself the end of this year would never come. So she accepted the offer which had been made to her. No sooner had she given her word to Ricky that she would marry him within one year from that very day, than she felt a complete change come over her. She found herself able to say all that she wished with the greatest ease, and to say it in an elegant, finished, and natural manner. She at once engaged Ricky in a brilliant and lengthy conversation, holding her own so well that Ricky feared he had given her a larger share of sense than he had retained for himself.

On her return to the palace amazement reigned throughout the Court at such a sudden and extraordinary change. Whereas formerly they had been accustomed to hear her give vent to silly, pert remarks, they now heard her express herself sensibly and very wittily.

The entire Court was overjoyed. The only person not too

pleased was the younger sister, for now that she had no longer the advantage over the elder in wit, she seemed nothing but a little fright in comparison.

The king himself often took her advice, and several times held his councils in her apartment.

The news of this change spread abroad, and the princes of the neighbouring kingdoms made many attempts to captivate her. Almost all asked her in marriage. But she found none with enough sense, and so she listened to all without promising herself to any.

At last came one who was so powerful, so rich, so witty, and so handsome, that she could not help being somewhat attracted by him. Her father noticed this, and told her she could make her own choice of a husband: she had only to declare herself.

Now the more sense one has, the more difficult it is to make up one's mind in an affair of this kind. After thanking her father, therefore, she asked for a little time to think it over.

In order to ponder quietly what she had better do she went to walk in a wood—the very one, as it happened, where she encountered Ricky of the Tuft.

While she walked, deep in thought, she heard beneath her feet a thudding sound, as though many people were running busily to and for. Listening more attentively she heard voices. "Bring me that boiler," said one; then another—"Put some wood on that fire!"

At that moment the ground opened, and she saw below what appeared to be a large kitchen full of cooks and scullions, and all the train of attendants which the preparation of a great banquet involves. A gang of some twenty or thirty spit-turners emerged and took up their positions round a very long table in a path in the wood. They all wore their cook's caps on one side, and with their basting implements in their hands they kept time together as they worked, to the lilt of a melodious song.

The princess was astonished by this spectacle, and asked for whom their work was being done.

"For Prince Ricky of the Tuft, madam," said the foreman of the gang; "his wedding is to-morrow."

At this the princess was more surprised than ever. In a flash she remembered that it was a year to the very day since she had promised to marry Prince Ricky of the Tuft, and was taken aback by the recollection. The reason she had forgotten was that when she made the promise she was still without sense, and with the acquisition of that intelligence which the prince had bestowed upon her, all memory of her former stupidities had been blotted out.

She had not gone another thirty paces when Ricky of the Tuft appeared before her, gallant and resplendent, like a prince upon his wedding day.

"As you see, madam," he said, "I keep my word to the minute. I do not doubt that you have come to keep yours, and by giving me your hand to make me the happiest of men."

"I will be frank with you," replied the princess. "I have not yet made up my mind on the point, and I am afraid I shall never be able to take the decision you desire."

"You astonish me, madam," said Ricky of the Tuft.

"I can well believe it," said the princess, "and undoubtedly, if I had to deal with a clown, or a man who lacked good sense, I should feel myself very awkwardly situated. 'A princess must keep

49

her word,' he would say, 'and you must marry me because you promised to!' But I am speaking to a man of the world, of the greatest good sense, and I am sure that he will listen to reason. As you are aware, I could not make up my mind to marry you even when I was entirely without sense; how can you expect that to-day, possessing the intelligence you bestowed on me, which makes me still more difficult to please than formerly, I should take a decision which I could not take then? If you wished so much to marry me, you were very wrong to relieve me of my stupidity, and to let me see more clearly than I did."

"If a man who lacked good sense," replied Ricky of the Tuft, "would be justified, as you have just said, in reproaching you for breaking your word, why do you expect, madam, that I should act differently where the happiness of my whole life is at stake? Is it reasonable that people who have sense should be treated worse than those who have none? Would you maintain that for a moment—you, who so markedly have sense, and desired so ardently to have it? But, pardon me, let us get to the facts. With the exception of my ugliness, is there anything about me which displeases you? Are you dissatisfied with my breeding, my brains, my disposition, or my manners?"

"In no way," replied the princess; "I like exceedingly all that you have displayed of the qualities you mention."

"In that case," said Ricky of the Tuft, "happiness will be mine, for it lies in your power to make me the most attractive of men."

"How can that be done?" asked the princess.

"It will happen of itself," replied Ricky of the Tuft, "if you love me well enough to wish that it be so. To remove your

Ricky of the Tuft

Away she went, beside herself with delight

Page 63

She opened the door of the room
Page 85

doubts, madam, let me tell you that the same fairy who on the day of my birth bestowed upon me the power of endowing with intelligence the woman of my choice, gave to you also the power of endowing with beauty the man whom you should love, and on whom you should wish to confer this favour."

"If that is so," said the princess, "I wish with all my heart that you may become the handsomest and most attractive prince in the world, and I give you without reserve the boon which it is mine to bestow."

No sooner had the princess uttered these words than Ricky of the Tuft appeared before her eyes as the handsomest, most graceful and attractive man that she had ever set eyes on.

Some people assert that this was not the work of fairy enchantment, but that love alone brought about the transformation. They say that the princess, as she mused upon her lover's constancy, upon his good sense, and his many admirable qualities of heart and head, grew blind to the deformity of his body and the ugliness of his face; that his hump back seemed no more than was natural in a man who could make the courtliest of bows, and that the dreadful limp which had formerly distressed her now betokened nothing more than a certain diffidence and charming deference of manner. They say further that she found his eyes shine all the brighter for their squint, and that this defect in them was to her but a sign of passionate love; while his great red nose she found nought but martial and heroic.

However that may be, the princess promised to marry him on the spot, provided only that he could obtain the consent of her royal father.

The king knew Ricky of the Tuft to be a prince both wise and witty, and on learning of his daughter's regard for him, he accepted him with pleasure as a son-in-law.

The wedding took place upon the morrow, just as Ricky of the Tuft had foreseen, and in accordance with the arrangements he had long ago put in train.

CINDERELLA

ONCE upon a time there was a worthy man who married for his second wife the haughtiest, proudest woman that had ever been seen. She had two daughters, who possessed their mother's temper and resembled her in everything. Her husband, on the other hand, had a young daughter, who was of an exceptionally sweet and gentle nature. She got this from her mother, who had been the nicest person in the world.

The wedding was no sooner over than the stepmother began to display her bad temper. She could not endure the excellent qualities of this young girl, for they made her own daughters appear more hateful than ever. She thrust upon her all the meanest tasks about the house. It was she who had to clean the plates and the stairs, and sweep out the rooms of the mistress of the house and her daughters. She slept on a wretched mattress in a garret at the top of the house, while the sisters had rooms with parquet flooring, and beds of the most fashionable style, with mirrors in which they could see themselves from top to toe.

The poor girl endured everything patiently, not daring to complain to her father. The latter would have scolded her, because he was entirely ruled by his wife. When she had finished her work she used to sit amongst the cinders in the corner of the chimney, and it was from this habit that she came to be commonly known as Cinder-maid. The younger of the two sisters, who was not quite so spiteful as the elder, called her Cinderella. But her wretched clothes did not prevent Cinderella from being a hundred times more beautiful than her sisters, for all their resplendent garments.

It happened that the king's son gave a ball, and he invited all persons of high degree. The two young ladies were invited amongst others, for they cut a considerable figure in the country. Not a little pleased were they, and the question of what clothes and what mode of dressing the hair would become them best took up all their time. And all this meant fresh trouble for Cinderella, for it was she who went over her sisters' linen and ironed their ruffles. They could talk of nothing else but the fashions in clothes.

"For my part," said the elder, "I shall wear my dress of red velvet, with the Honiton lace."

"I have only my everyday petticoat," said the younger, "but to make up for it I shall wear my cloak with the golden flowers and my necklace of diamonds, which are not so bad."

They sent for a good hairdresser to arrange their doublefrilled caps, and bought patches at the best shop.

They summoned Cinderella and asked her advice, for she had good taste. Cinderella gave them the best possible suggestions, and even offered to dress their hair, to which they gladly agreed.

While she was thus occupied they said:

"Cinderella, would you not like to go to the ball?"

"Ah, but you fine young ladies are laughing at me. It would be no place for me."

"That is very true, people would laugh to see a cinder-maid in the ballroom."

Any one else but Cinderella would have done their hair amiss, but she was good-natured, and she finished them off to perfection.

The haughtiest, proudest woman that had ever been seen

Cinderella

They were so excited in their glee that for nearly two days they ate nothing. They broke more than a dozen laces through drawing their stays tight in order to make their waists more slender, and they were perpetually in front of a mirror.

At last the happy day arrived. Away they went, Cinderella watching them as long as she could keep them in sight. When she could no longer see them she began to cry. Her godmother found her in tears, and asked what was troubling her.

"I should like—I should like——"

She was crying so bitterly that she could not finish the sentence.

Said her godmother, who was a fairy:

"You would like to go to the ball, would you not?"

"Ah, yes," said Cinderella, sighing.

"Well, well," said her godmother, "promise to be a good girl and I will arrange for you to go."

She took Cinderella into her room and said:

"Go into the garden and bring me a pumpkin."

Cinderella went at once and gathered the finest that she could find. This she brought to her godmother, wondering how a pumpkin could help in taking her to the ball.

Her godmother scooped it out, and when only the rind was left, struck it with her wand. Instantly the pumpkin was changed into a beautiful coach, gilded all over.

Then she went and looked in the mouse-trap, where she found six mice all alive. She told Cinderella to lift the door of the mouse-trap a little, and as each mouse came out she gave it a tap with her wand, whereupon it was transformed into a fine horse. So that here was a fine team of six dappled mouse-grey horses.

Cinderella

But she was puzzled to know how to provide a coachman.

"I will go and see," said Cinderella, "if there is not a rat in the rat-trap. We could make a coachman of him."

"Quite right," said her godmother, "go and see."

Cinderella brought in the rat-trap, which contained three big rats. The fairy chose one specially on account of his elegant whiskers.

As soon as she had touched him he turned into a fat coachman with the finest moustachios that ever were seen.

"Now go into the garden and bring me the six lizards which you will find behind the water-butt."

No sooner had they been brought than the godmother turned them into six lackeys, who at once climbed up behind the coach in their braided liveries, and hung on there as if they had never done anything else all their lives.

Then said the fairy godmother:

"Well, there you have the means of going to the ball. Are you satisfied?"

"Oh, yes, but am I to go like this in my ugly clothes?"

Her godmother merely touched her with her wand, and on the instant her clothes were changed into garments of gold and silver cloth, bedecked with jewels. After that her godmother gave her a pair of glass slippers, the prettiest in the world.

Thus altered, she entered the coach. Her godmother bade her not to stay beyond midnight whatever happened, warning her that if she remained at the ball a moment longer, her coach would again become a pumpkin, her horses mice, and her lackeys lizards, while her old clothes would reappear upon her once more.

Her godmother found her in tears

Cinderella

She promised her godmother that she would not fail to leave the ball before midnight, and away she went, beside herself with delight.

Away she went

The king's son, when he was told of the arrival of a great princess whom nobody knew, went forth to receive her. He handed her down from the coach, and led her into the hall where the company was assembled. At once there fell a great silence. The dancers stopped, the violins played no more, so rapt was the attention which everybody bestowed upon the superb beauty of the unknown guest. Everywhere could be heard in confused whispers:

"Oh, how beautiful she is!"

The king, old man as he was, could not take his eyes off her, and whispered to the queen that it was many a long day since he had seen any one so beautiful and charming.

All the ladies were eager to scrutinise her clothes and the dressing of her hair, being determined to copy them on the morrow, provided they could find materials so fine, and tailors so clever.

The king's son placed her in the seat of honour, and at once begged the privilege of being her partner in a dance. Such was the grace with which she danced that the admiration of all was increased.

A magnificent supper was served, but the young prince could eat nothing, so taken up was he with watching her. She went and sat beside her sisters, and bestowed numberless attentions upon them. She made them share with her the oranges and lemons which the king had given her—greatly to their astonishment, for they did not recognise her.

While they were talking, Cinderella heard the clock strike a quarter to twelve. She at once made a profound curtsey to the company, and departed as quickly as she could.

As soon as she was home again she sought out her godmother, and having thanked her, declared that she wished to go upon the morrow once more to the ball, because the king's son had invited her.

While she was busy telling her godmother all that had happened at the ball, her two sisters knocked at the door. Cinderella let them in.

"What a long time you have been coming!" she declared, rubbing her eyes and stretching herself as if she had only just awakened. In real truth she had not for a moment wished to sleep since they had left.

"If you had been at the ball," said one of the sisters, "you would not be feeling weary. There came a most beautiful princess, the most beautiful that has ever been seen, and she bestowed numberless attentions upon us, and gave us her oranges and lemons."

Cinderella was overjoyed. She asked them the name of the princess, but they replied that no one knew it, and that the king's

She rose and fled as nimbly as a fawn

Cinderella

son was so distressed that he would give anything in the world to know who she was.

Cinderella smiled, and said she must have been beautiful indeed.

"Oh, how lucky you are. Could I not manage to see her? Oh, please, Javotte, lend me the yellow dress which you wear every day."

"Indeed!" said Javotte, "that is a fine idea. Lend my dress to a grubby cinder-maid like you—you must think me mad!"

Cinderella had expected this refusal. She was in no way upset, for she would have been very greatly embarrassed had her sister been willing to lend the dress.

The next day the two sisters went to the ball, and so did Cinderella, even more splendidly attired than the first time.

The king's son was always at her elbow, and paid her endless compliments.

The young girl enjoyed herself so much that she forgot her godmother's bidding completely, and when the first stroke of midnight fell upon her ears, she thought it was no more than eleven o'clock.

She rose and fled as nimbly as a fawn. The prince followed her, but could not catch her. She let fall one of her glass slippers, however, and this the prince picked up with tender care.

When Cinderella reached home she was out of breath, without coach, without lackeys, and in her shabby clothes. Nothing remained of all her splendid clothes save one of the little slippers, the fellow to the one which she had let fall.

Inquiries were made of the palace doorkeepers as to whether they had seen a princess go out, but they declared they had seen no one leave except a young girl, very ill-clad, who looked more like a peasant than a young lady.

When her two sisters returned from the ball, Cinderella asked them if they had again enjoyed themselves, and if the beautiful lady had been there. They told her that she was present, but had fled away when midnight sounded, and in such haste that she had let fall one of her little glass slippers, the prettiest thing in the world. They added that the king's son, who picked it up, had done nothing but gaze at it for the rest of the ball, from which it was plain that he was deeply in love with its beautiful owner.

They spoke the truth. A few days later, the king's son caused a proclamation to be made by trumpeters, that he would take for wife the owner of the foot which the slipper would fit.

They tried it first on the princesses, then on the duchesses and the whole of the Court, but in vain. Presently they brought it to the home of the two sisters, who did all they could to squeeze a foot into the slipper. This, however, they could not manage.

Cinderella was looking on and recognised her slipper:

"Let me see," she cried, laughingly, "if it will not fit me."

Her sisters burst out laughing, and began to gibe at her, but the equerry who was trying on the slipper looked closely at Cinderella. Observing that she was very beautiful he declared that the claim was quite a fair one, and that his orders were to try the slipper on every maiden. He bade Cinderella sit down, and on putting the slipper to her little foot he perceived that the latter slid in without trouble, and was moulded to its shape like wax.

Great was the astonishment of the two sisters at this, and greater still when Cinderella drew from her pocket the other little slipper. This she likewise drew on.

They tried it first on the princesses

Cinderella

At that very moment her godmother appeared on the scene. She gave a tap with her wand to Cinderella's clothes, and transformed them into a dress even more magnificent than her previous ones.

The two sisters recognised her for the beautiful person whom they had seen at the ball, and threw themselves at her feet, begging her pardon for all the ill-treatment she had suffered at their hands.

Cinderella raised them, and declaring as she embraced them that she pardoned them with all her heart, bade them to love her well in future.

She was taken to the palace of the young prince in all her new array. He found her more beautiful than ever, and was married to her a few days afterwards.

Cinderella was as good as she was beautiful. She set aside apartments in the palace for her two sisters, and married them the very same day to two gentlemen of high rank about the Court.

LITTLE RED RIDING HOOD

ONCE upon a time there was a little village girl, the prettiest that had ever been seen. Her mother doted on her. Her grandmother was even fonder, and made her a little red hood, which became her so well that everywhere she went by the name of Little Red Riding Hood.

One day her mother, who had just made and baked some cakes, said to her:

"Go and see how your grandmother is, for I have been told that she is ill. Take her a cake and this little pot of butter."

Little Red Riding Hood set off at once for the house of her grandmother, who lived in another village.

On her way through a wood she met old Father Wolf. He would have very much liked to eat her, but dared not do so on account of some wood-cutters who were in the forest. He asked her where she was going. The poor child, not knowing that it was dangerous to stop and listen to a wolf, said:

"I am going to see my grandmother, and am taking her a cake and a pot of butter which my mother has sent to her."

"Does she live far away?" asked the Wolf.

"Oh yes," replied Little Red Riding Hood; "it is yonder by the mill which you can see right below there, and it is the first house in the village."

"Well now," said the Wolf, "I think I shall go and see her too.

Little Red Riding Hood

I will go by this path, and you by that path, and we will see who gets there first."

She met old Father Wolf

The Wolf set off running with all his might by the shorter road, and the little girl continued on her way by the longer road. As she went she amused herself by gathering nuts, running after the butterflies, and making nosegays of the wild flowers which she found.

The Wolf was not long in reaching the grandmother's house. He knocked. *Toc Toc.*

Little Red Riding Hood

"Who is there?"

"It is your little daughter, Red Riding Hood," said the Wolf, disguising his voice, "and I bring you a cake and a little pot of butter as a present from my mother."

Making nosegays of the wild flowers

The worthy grandmother was in bed, not being very well, and cried out to him:

"Pull out the peg and the latch will fall."

The Wolf drew out the peg and the door flew open. Then he sprang upon the poor old lady and ate her up in less than no time, for he had been more than three days without food.

Little Red Riding Hood

After that he shut the door, lay down in the grandmother's bed, and waited for Little Red Riding Hood.

Presently she came and knocked. *Toc Toc.*

"Who is there?"

Come up on the bed with me

Now Little Red Riding Hood on hearing the Wolf's gruff voice was at first frightened, but thinking that her grandmother had a bad cold, she replied:

"It is your little daughter, Red Riding Hood, and I bring you cake and a little pot of butter from my mother."

Softening his voice, the Wolf called out to her:

Little Red Riding Hood

"Pull out the peg and the latch will fall."

Little Red Riding Hood drew out the peg and the door flew open.

When he saw her enter, the Wolf hid himself in the bed beneath the counterpane.

"Put the cake and the little pot of butter on the bin," he said, "and come up on the bed with me."

Little Red Riding Hood took off her clothes, but when she climbed up on the bed she was astonished to see how her grandmother looked in her nightgown.

"Grandmother dear!" she exclaimed, "what big arms you have!"

"The better to embrace you, my child!"

"Grandmother dear, what big legs you have!"

"The better to run with, my child!"

"Grandmother dear, what big ears you have!"

"The better to hear with, my child!"

"Grandmother dear, what big eyes you have!"

"The better to see with, my child!"

"Grandmother dear, what big teeth you have!"

"The better to eat you with!"

With these words the wicked Wolf leapt upon Little Red Riding Hood. He was just about to gobble her up when a hunter who had earlier seen the Wolf pass by in the direction of the cottage, burst through the door and saved her from certain death.

BLUE BEARD

ONCE upon a time there was a man who owned splendid town and country houses, gold and silver plate, tapestries and coaches gilt all over. But the poor fellow had a blue beard, and this made him so ugly and frightful that there was not a woman or girl who did not run away at sight of him.

Amongst his neighbours was a lady of high degree who had two surpassingly beautiful daughters. He asked for the hand of one of these in marriage, leaving it to their mother to choose which should be bestowed upon him. Both girls, however, raised objections, and his offer was bandied from one to the other, neither being able to bring herself to accept a man with a blue beard. Another reason for their distaste was the fact that he had already married several wives, and no one knew what had become of them.

In order that they might become better acquainted, Blue Beard invited the two girls, with their mother and three or four of their best friends, to meet a party of young men from the neighbourhood at one of his country houses. Here they spent eight whole days, and throughout their stay there was a constant round of picnics, hunting and fishing expeditions, dances, dinners, and luncheons; and they never slept at all, through spending all the night in playing merry pranks upon each other. In short, everything went so gaily that the younger daughter began to think the master of the house had not so very blue a beard after all, and that he was an exceedingly agreeable man. As soon as the party returned to town their marriage took place.

At the end of a month Blue Beard informed his wife that important business obliged him to make a journey into a distant part of the country, which would occupy at least six weeks. He begged her to amuse herself well during his absence, and suggested that she should invite some of her friends and take them, if she liked, to the country. He was particularly anxious that she should enjoy herself thoroughly.

"Here," he said, "are the keys of the two large storerooms, and here is the one that locks up the gold and silver plate which is not in everyday use. This key belongs to the strong-boxes where my gold and silver is kept, this to the caskets containing my jewels; while here you have the master-key which gives admittance to all the apartments. As regards this little key, it is the key of the small room at the end of the long passage on the lower floor. You may open everything, you may go everywhere, but I forbid you to enter this little room. And I forbid you so seriously that if you were indeed to open the door, I should be so angry that I might do anything."

She promised to follow out these instructions exactly, and after embracing her, Blue Beard stepped into his coach and was off upon his journey.

Her neighbours and friends did not wait to be invited before coming to call upon the young bride, so great was their eagerness to see the splendours of her house. They had not dared to venture

Blue Beard

Every evening the Beast paid her a visit
Page 110

Could your father but see you, my poor child
Page 132

Blue Beard

while her husband was there, for his blue beard frightened them. But in less than no time there they were, running in and out of the rooms, the closets, and the wardrobes, each of which was finer than the last. Presently they went upstairs to the storerooms, and there they could not admire enough the profusion and magnificence of the tapestries, beds, sofas, cabinets, tables, and stands. There were mirrors in which they could view themselves from top to toe, some with frames of plate glass, others with frames of silver and gilt lacquer, that were the most superb and beautiful things that had ever been seen. They were loud and persistent in their envy of their friend's good fortune. She, on the other hand, derived little amusement from the sight of all these riches, the reason being that she was impatient to go and inspect the little room on the lower floor.

So overcome with curiosity was she that, without reflecting upon the discourtesy of leaving her guests, she ran down a private staircase, so precipitately that twice or thrice she nearly broke her neck, and so reached the door of the little room. There she paused for a while, thinking of the prohibition which her husband had made, and reflecting that harm might come to her as a result of disobedience. But the temptation was so great that she could not conquer it. Taking the little key, with a trembling hand she opened the door of the room.

At first she saw nothing, for the windows were closed, but after a few moments she perceived dimly that the floor was entirely covered with blood, and that in the blood were reflected the bodies of several women that hung along the walls. These were all the wives of Blue Beard, whom he had slain, one after another.

Blue Beard

She thought to die of terror, and the key of the room, which she had just withdrawn from the lock, fell from her hand.

When she had somewhat regained her senses, she picked up the key, closed the door, and went up to her chamber to compose

She washed it well

herself a little. But this she could not do, for her nerves were too shaken. Noticing that the key of the little room was stained with blood, she wiped it two or three times. But the blood did not go. She washed it well, and even rubbed it with sand and grit. Always the blood remained. For the key was bewitched, and there was no means of cleaning it completely. When the blood was removed from one side, it reappeared on the other.

Blue Beard returned from his journey that very evening. He had received some letters on the way, he said, from which he learned that the business upon which he had set forth had just been concluded to his satisfaction. His wife did everything she could to make it appear that she was delighted by his speedy return.

86

Sister Anne

Blue Beard

On the morrow he demanded the keys. She gave them to him, but with so trembling a hand that he guessed at once what had happened.

"How comes it," he said to her, "that the key of the little room is not with the others?"

"I must have left it upstairs upon my table," she said.

"Do not fail to bring it to me presently," said Blue Beard.

After several delays the key had to be brought. Blue Beard examined it, and addressed his wife.

"Why is there blood on this key?"

"I do not know at all," replied the poor woman, paler than death.

"You do not know at all?" exclaimed Blue Beard; "I know well enough. You wanted to enter the little room! Well, madam, enter it you shall—you shall go and take your place among the ladies you have seen there."

She threw herself at her husband's feet, asking his pardon with tears, and with all the signs of a true repentance for her disobedience. She would have softened a rock, in her beauty and distress, but Blue Beard had a heart harder than any stone.

"You must die, madam," he said; "and at once."

"Since I must die," she replied, gazing at him with eyes that were wet with tears, "give me a little time to say my prayers."

"I give you one quarter of an hour," replied Blue Beard, "but not a moment longer."

When the poor girl was alone, she called her sister to her and said:

"Sister Anne"—for that was her name—"go up, I implore you, to the top of the tower, and see if my brothers are not

89

approaching. They promised that they would come and visit me to-day. If you see them, make signs to them to hasten."

Sister Anne went up to the top of the tower, and the poor unhappy girl cried out to her from time to time:

"Anne, Sister Anne, do you see nothing coming?"

And Sister Anne replied:

"I see nought but dust in the sun and the green grass growing."

Presently Blue Beard, grasping a great cutlass, cried out at the top of his voice:

"Come down quickly, or I shall come upstairs myself."

"Oh please, one moment more," called out his wife.

And at the same moment she cried in a whisper:

"Anne, Sister Anne, do you see nothing coming?"

"I see nought but dust in the sun and the green grass growing."

"Come down at once, I say," shouted Blue Beard, "or I will come upstairs myself."

"I am coming," replied his wife.

The she called:

"Anne, Sister Anne, do you see nothing coming?"

"I see," replied Sister Anne, "a great cloud of dust which comes this way."

"Is it my brothers?"

"Alas, sister, no; it is but a flock of sheep."

"Do you refuse to come down?" roared Blue Beard.

"One little moment more," exclaimed his wife.

Once more she cried:

"Anne, Sister Anne, do you see nothing coming?"

90

Brandishing the cutlass aloft

Blue Beard

"I see," replied her sister, "two horsemen who come this way, but they are as yet a long way off. . . . Heaven be praised," she exclaimed a moment later, "they are my brothers. . . . I am signalling to them all I can to hasten."

Blue Beard let forth so mighty a shout that the whole house shook. The poor wife went down and cast herself at his feet, all dishevelled and in tears.

"That avails you nothing," said Blue Beard; "you must die."

Seizing her by the hair with one hand, and with the other brandishing the cutlass aloft, he made as if to cut off her head.

The poor woman, turning towards him and fixing a dying gaze upon him, begged for a brief moment in which to collect her thoughts.

"No! no!" he cried; "commend your soul to Heaven." And raising his arm——

At this very moment there came so loud a knocking at the gate that Blue Beard stopped short. The gate was opened, and two horsemen dashed in, who drew their swords and rode straight at Blue Beard. The latter recognised them as the brothers of his wife —one of them a dragoon, and the other a musketeer—and fled instantly in an effort to escape. But the two brothers were so close upon him that they caught him ere he could gain the first flight of steps. They plunged their swords through his body and left him dead. The poor woman was nearly as dead as her husband, and had not the strength to rise and embrace her brothers.

It was found that Blue Beard had no heirs, and that consequently his wife became mistress of all his wealth. She devoted a portion to arranging a marriage between her sister Anne and a young gentleman with whom the latter had been for some time in

Blue Beard

love, while another portion purchased a captain's commission for each of her brothers. The rest formed a dowry for her own marriage with a very worthy man, who banished from her mind all memory of the evil days she had spent with Blue Beard.

BEAUTY AND THE BEAST

ONCE upon a time there lived a merchant who was exceedingly rich. He had six children—three boys and three girls—and being a sensible man he spared no expense upon their education, but engaged tutors of every kind for them. All his daughters were pretty, but the youngest especially was admired by everybody. When she was small she was known simply as "the little beauty," and this name stuck to her, causing a great deal of jealousy on the part of her sisters.

This youngest girl was not only prettier than her sisters, but very much nicer. The two elder girls were very arrogant as a result of their wealth; they pretended to be great ladies, declining to receive the daughters of other merchants, and associating only with people of quality. Every day they went off to balls and theatres, and for walks in the park, with many a gibe at their little sister, who spent much of her time in reading good books.

Now these girls were known to be very rich, and in consequence were sought in marriage by many prominent merchants. The two eldest said they would never marry unless they could find a duke, or at least a count. But Beauty—this, as I have mentioned, was the name by which the youngest was known—very politely thanked all who proposed marriage to her, and said that she was too young at present, and that she wished to keep her father company for several years yet.

95

Beauty and the Beast

Suddenly the merchant lost his fortune, the sole property which remained to him being a small house in the country, a long way from the capital. With tears he broke it to his children that they would have to move to this house, where by working like peasants they might just be able to live.

The two elder girls replied that they did not wish to leave the town, and that they had several admirers who would be only too happy to marry them, notwithstanding their loss of fortune. But the simple maidens were mistaken: their admirers would no longer look at them, now that they were poor. Everybody disliked them on account of their arrogance, and folks declared that they did not deserve pity: in fact, that it was a good thing their pride had had a fall—a turn at minding sheep would teach them how to play the fine lady! "But we are very sorry for Beauty's misfortune," everybody added; "she is such a dear girl, and was always so considerate to poor people: so gentle, and with such charming manners!"

There were even several worthy men who would have married her, despite the fact that she was now penniless; but she told them she could not make up her mind to leave her poor father in his misfortune, and that she intended to go with him to the country, to comfort him and help him to work. Poor Beauty had been very grieved at first over the loss of her fortune, but she said to herself:

"However much I cry, I shall not recover my wealth, so I must try to be happy without it."

When they were established in the country the merchant and his family started working on the land. Beauty used to rise at four o'clock in the morning, and was busy all day looking after the house, and preparing dinner for the family. At first she found it

very hard, for she was not accustomed to work like a servant, but
at the end of a couple of months she grew stronger, and her health

At first she found it very hard

was improved by the work. When she had leisure she read, or
played the harpsichord, or sang at her spinning-wheel.

Her two sisters, on the other hand, were bored to death; they
did not get up till ten o'clock in the morning, and they idled about
all day. Their only diversion was to bemoan the beautiful clothes
they used to wear and the company they used to keep. "Look at
our little sister," they would say to each other; "her tastes are so

low and her mind so stupid that she is quite content with this miserable state of affairs."

The good merchant did not share the opinion of his two daughters, for he knew that Beauty was more fitted to shine in company than her sisters. He was greatly impressed by the girl's good qualities, and especially by her patience—for her sisters, not content with leaving her all the work of the house, never missed an opportunity of insulting her.

They had been living for a year in this seclusion when the merchant received a letter informing him that a ship on which he had some merchandise had just come safely home. The news nearly turned the heads of the two elder girls, for they thought that at last they would be able to quit their dull life in the country. When they saw their father ready to set out they begged him to bring them back dresses, furs, caps, and finery of every kind. Beauty asked for nothing, thinking to herself that all the money which the merchandise might yield would not be enough to satisfy her sisters' demands.

"You have not asked me for anything," said her father.

"As you are so kind as to think of me," she replied, "please bring me a rose, for there are none here."

Beauty had no real craving for a rose, but she was anxious not to seem to disparage the conduct of her sisters. The latter would have declared that she purposely asked for nothing in order to be different from them.

The merchant duly set forth; but when he reached his destination there was a law-suit over his merchandise, and after much trouble he returned poorer than he had been before. With only thirty miles to go before reaching home, he was already looking

Look at our little sister

forward to the pleasure of seeing his children again, when he found he had to pass through a large wood. Here he lost himself. It was snowing horribly; the wind was so strong that twice he was

It was snowing horribly

thrown from his horse, and when night came on he made up his mind he must either die of hunger and cold or be eaten by the wolves that he could hear howling all about him.

Suddenly he saw, at the end of a long avenue of trees, a strong light. It seemed to be some distance away, but he walked towards it, and presently discovered that it came from a large palace, which was all lit up.

The merchant thanked heaven for sending him this help, and hastened to the castle. To his surprise, however, he found no one about in the courtyards. His horse, which had followed him, saw a large stable open and went in; and on finding hay and oats in readiness the poor animal, which was dying of hunger, set to with a will. The merchant tied him up in the stable, and approached the house, where he found not a soul. He entered a large room; here there was a good fire, and a table laden with food, but with a place laid for one only. The rain and snow had soaked him to the skin, so he drew near the fire to dry himself. "I am sure," he remarked to himself, "that the master of this house or his servants will forgive the liberty I am taking; doubtless they will be here soon."

He waited some considerable time; but eleven o'clock struck and still he had seen nobody. Being no longer able to resist his hunger he took a chicken and devoured it in two mouthfuls, trembling. Then he drank several glasses of wine, and becoming bolder ventured out of the room. He went through several magnificently furnished apartments, and finally found a room with a very good bed. It was now past midnight, and as he was very tired he decided to shut the door and go to bed.

It was ten o'clock the next morning when he rose, and he was greatly astonished to find a new suit in place of his own, which had been spoilt. "This palace," he said to himself, "must surely belong to some good fairy, who has taken pity on my plight."

He looked out of the window. The snow had vanished, and his eyes rested instead upon arbours of flowers—a charming spectacle. He went back to the room where he had supped the night before, and found there a little table with a cup of chocolate on it. "I thank you, Madam Fairy," he said aloud, "for being so kind as to think of my breakfast."

Having drunk his chocolate the good man went forth to look for his horse. As he passed under a bower of roses he remembered that Beauty had asked for one, and he plucked a spray from a mass of blooms. The very same moment he heard a terrible noise, and saw a beast coming towards him which was so hideous that he came near to fainting.

"Ungrateful wretch!" said the Beast, in a dreadful voice; "I have saved your life by receiving you into my castle, and in return for my trouble you steal that which I love better than anything in the world—my roses. You shall pay for this with your life! I give you fifteen minutes to make your peace with Heaven."

The merchant threw himself on his knees and wrung his hands. "Pardon, my lord!" he cried; "one of my daughters had asked for a rose, and I did not dream I should be giving offence by picking one."

"I am not called 'my lord,' " answered the monster, "but 'The Beast.' I have no liking for compliments, but prefer people to say what they think. Do not hope therefore to soften me by flattery. You have daughters, you say; well, I am willing to pardon you if one of your daughters will come, of her own choice, to die in your place. Do not argue with me—go! And swear that if your daughters refuse to die in your place you will come back again in three months."

The good man had no intention of sacrificing one of his daughters to this hideous monster, but he thought that at least he might have the pleasure of kissing them once again. He therefore swore to return, and the Beast told him he could go when he wished. "I do not wish you to go empty-handed," he added; "re-

The Beast

turn to the room where you slept; you will find there a large empty box. Fill it with what you will; I will have it sent home for you."

With these words the Beast withdrew, leaving the merchant to reflect that if he must indeed die, at all events he would have the consolation of providing for his poor children.

He went back to the room where he had slept. He found there a large number of gold pieces, and with these he filled the box the Beast had mentioned. Having closed the latter, he took his horse, which was still in the stable, and set forth from the palace, as melancholy now as he had been joyous when he entered it.

The horse of its own accord took one of the forest roads, and in a few hours the good man reached his own little house. His children crowded round him, but at sight of them, instead of welcoming their caresses, he burst into tears. In his hand was the bunch of roses which he had brought for Beauty, and he gave it to her with these words:

"Take these roses, Beauty; it is dearly that your poor father will have to pay for them."

Thereupon he told his family of the dire adventure which had befallen him. On hearing the tale the two elder girls were in a great commotion, and began to upbraid Beauty for not weeping as they did. "See to what her smugness has brought this young chit," they said; "surely she might strive to find some way out of this trouble, as we do! But oh, dear me, no; her ladyship is so determined to be different that she can speak of her father's death without a tear!"

"It would be quite useless to weep," said Beauty. "Why should I lament my father's death? He is not going to die. Since the monster agrees to accept a daughter instead, I intend to offer myself to appease his fury. It will be a happiness to do so, for in dying I shall have the joy of saving my father, and of proving to him my devotion."

"No, sister," said her three brothers; "you shall not die; we will go in quest of this monster, and will perish under his blows if we cannot kill him."

"Do not entertain any such hopes, my children," said the merchant; "the power of this Beast is so great that I have not the slightest expectation of escaping him. I am touched by the goodness of Beauty's heart, but I will not expose her to death. I am old and have not much longer to live; and I shall merely lose a few years that will be regretted only on account of you, my dear children."

"I can assure you, father," said Beauty, "that you will not go to this palace without me. You cannot prevent me from following you. Although I am young I am not so very deeply in love with life, and I would rather be devoured by this monster than die of the grief which your loss would cause me." Words were useless. Beauty was quite determined to go to this wonderful palace, and her sisters were not sorry, for they regarded her good qualities with deep jealousy.

The merchant was so taken up with the sorrow of losing his daughter that he forgot all about the box which he had filled with gold. To his astonishment, when he had shut the door of his room and was about to retire for the night, there it was at the side of his bed! He decided not to tell his children that he had become so rich, for his elder daughters would have wanted to go back to town, and he had resolved to die in the country. He did confide his secret to Beauty, however, and the latter told him that during his absence they had entertained some visitors, amongst whom were two admirers of her sisters. She begged her father to let them marry; for she was of such a sweet nature that she loved them, and forgave them with all her heart the evil they had done her.

When Beauty set off with her father the two heartless girls rubbed their eyes with an onion, so as to seem tearful; but her brothers wept in reality, as did also the merchant. Beauty alone did not cry, because she did not want to add to their sorrow.

Beauty and the Beast

The horse took the road to the palace, and by evening they espied it, all lit up as before. An empty stable awaited the nag, and when the good merchant and his daughter entered the great hall, they found there a table magnificently laid for two people. The merchant had not the heart to eat, but Beauty, forcing herself to appear calm, sat down and served him. Since the Beast had provided such splendid fare, she thought to herself, he must presumably be anxious to fatten her up before eating her.

When they had finished supper they heard a terrible noise. With tears the merchant bade farewell to his daughter, for he knew it was the Beast. Beauty herself could not help trembling at the awful apparition, but she did her best to compose herself. The Beast asked her if she had come of her own free will, and she timidly answered that such was the case.

"You are indeed kind," said the Beast, "and I am much obliged to you. You, my good man, will depart to-morrow morning, and you must not think of coming back again. Good-bye, Beauty!"

"Good-bye, Beast!" she answered.

Thereupon the monster suddenly disappeared.

"Daughter," said the merchant, embracing Beauty, "I am nearly dead with fright. Let me be the one to stay here!"

"No, father," said Beauty, firmly, "you must go to-morrow morning, and leave me to the mercy of Heaven. Perhaps pity will be taken on me."

They retired to rest, thinking they would not sleep at all during the night, but they were hardly in bed before their eyes were closed in sleep. In her dreams there appeared to Beauty a lady, who said to her:

"Your virtuous character pleases me, Beauty. In thus undertak-

ing to give your life to save your father you have performed an
act of goodness which shall not go unrewarded."

When she woke up Beauty related this dream to her father. He
was somewhat consoled by it, but could not refrain from loudly
giving vent to his grief when the time came to tear himself away
from his beloved child.

As soon as he had gone Beauty sat down in the great hall and
began to cry. But she had plenty of courage, and after imploring
divine protection she determined to grieve no more during the
short time she had yet to live.

She was convinced that the Beast would devour her that night,
but made up her mind that in the interval she would walk about
and have a look at this beautiful castle, the splendour of which she
could not but admire.

Imagine her surprise when she came upon a door on which
were the words "Beauty's Room!" She quickly opened this door,
and was dazzled by the magnificence of the appointments within.
"They are evidently anxious that I should not be dull," she murmured, as she caught sight of a large book-case, a harpsichord, and
several volumes of music. A moment later another thought crossed
her mind. "If I had only a day to spend here," she reflected, "such
provision would surely not have been made for me."

This notion gave her fresh courage. She opened the bookcase,
and found a book in which was written, in letters of gold:

"Ask for anything you wish: you are mistress of all here."

"Alas!" she said with a sigh, "my only wish is to see my poor
father, and to know what he is doing."

As she said this to herself she glanced at a large mirror. Imagine her astonishment when she perceived her home reflected in it,

and saw her father just approaching. Sorrow was written on his face; but when her sisters came to meet him it was impossible not to detect, despite the grimaces with which they tried to simulate grief, the satisfaction they felt at the loss of their sister. In a moment the vision faded away, yet Beauty could not but think that the Beast was very kind, and that she had nothing much to fear from him.

At midday she found the table laid, and during her meal she enjoyed an excellent concert, though the performers were invisible. But in the evening, as she was about to sit down at the table, she heard the noise made by the Beast, and quaked in spite of herself.

"Beauty," said the monster to her, "may I watch you have your supper?"

"You are master here," said the trembling Beauty.

"Not so," replied the Beast; "it is you who are mistress; you have only to tell me to go, if my presence annoys you, and I will go immediately. Tell me, now, do you not consider me very ugly?"

"I do," said Beauty, "since I must speak the truth; but I think you are also very kind."

"It is as you say," said the monster; "and in addition to being ugly, I lack intelligence. As I am well aware, I am a mere beast."

"It is not the way with stupid people," answered Beauty, "to admit a lack of intelligence. Fools never realise it."

"Sup well, Beauty," said the monster, "and try to banish dullness from your home—for all about you is yours, and I should be sorry to think you were not happy."

"You are indeed kind," said Beauty. "With one thing, I must

own, I am well pleased, and that is your kind heart. When I think of that you no longer seem to be ugly."

"Oh yes," answered the Beast, "I have a good heart, right enough, but I am a monster."

"There are many men," said Beauty, "who make worse monsters than you, and I prefer you, notwithstanding your looks, to those who under the semblance of men hide false, corrupt, and ungrateful hearts."

The Beast replied that if only he had a grain of wit he would compliment her in the grand style by way of thanks; but that being so stupid he could only say he was much obliged.

Beauty ate with a good appetite, for she now had scarcely any fear of the Beast. But she nearly died of fright when he put this question to her:

"Beauty, will you be my wife?"

For some time she did not answer, fearing lest she might anger the monster by her refusal. She summoned up courage at last to say, rather fearfully, "No, Beast!"

The poor monster gave forth so terrible a sigh that the noise of it went whistling through the whole palace. But to Beauty's speedy relief the Beast sadly took his leave and left the room, turning several times as he did so to look once more at her. Left alone, Beauty was moved by great compassion for this poor Beast. "What a pity he is so ugly," she said, "for he is so good."

Beauty passed three months in the palace quietly enough. Every evening the Beast paid her a visit, and entertained her at supper by a display of much good sense, if not with what the world calls wit. And every day Beauty was made aware of fresh kindnesses on the part of the monster. Through seeing him often she had become accustomed to his ugliness, and far from dreading the moment of his visit, she frequently looked at her watch to see if it was nine o'clock, the hour when the Beast always appeared.

One thing alone troubled Beauty; every evening, before retiring to bed, the monster asked her if she would be his wife, and seemed overwhelmed with grief when she refused. One day she said to him:

"You distress me, Beast. I wish I could marry you, but I cannot deceive you by allowing you to believe that that can ever be. I will always be your friend—be content with that."

"Needs must," said the Beast. "But let me make the position plain. I know I am very terrible, but I love you very much, and I shall be very happy if you will only remain here. Promise that you will never leave me."

Beauty blushed at these words. She had seen in her mirror that her father was stricken down by the sorrow of having lost her, and she wished very much to see him again. "I would willingly promise to remain with you always," she said to the Beast, "but I have so great a desire to see my father again that I shall die of grief if you refuse me this boon."

"I would rather die myself than cause you grief," said the monster. "I will send you back to your father. You shall stay with him, and your Beast shall die of sorrow at your departure."

"No, no," said Beauty, crying; "I like you too much to wish to cause your death. I promise you I will return in eight days. You have shown me that my sisters are married, and that my brothers have joined the army. My father is all alone; let me stay with him one week."

"You shall be with him to-morrow morning," said the Beast.

Beauty and the Beast

"But remember your promise. All you have to do when you want to return is to put your ring on a table when you are going to bed. Good-bye, Beauty!"

As usual, the Beast sighed when he said these last words, and Beauty went to bed quite down-hearted at having grieved him.

When she woke the next morning she found she was in her father's house. She rang a little bell which stood by the side of her bed, and it was answered by their servant, who gave a great cry at sight of her. The good man came running at the noise, and was overwhelmed with joy at the sight of his dear daughter. Their embraces lasted for more than a quarter of an hour. When their transports had subsided, it occurred to Beauty that she had no clothes to put on; but the servant told her that she had just discovered in the next room a chest full of dresses trimmed with gold and studded with diamonds. Beauty felt grateful to the Beast for this attention, and having selected the simplest of the gowns she bade the servant pack up the others, as she wished to send them as presents to her sisters. The words were hardly out of her mouth when the chest disappeared. Her father expressed the opinion that the Beast wished her to keep them all for herself, and in a trice dresses and chest were back again where they were before.

When Beauty had dressed she learned that her sisters, with their husbands, had arrived. Both were very unhappy. The eldest had wedded an exceedingly handsome man, but the latter was so taken up with his own looks that he studied them from morning to night, and despised his wife's beauty. The second had married a man with plenty of brains, but he only used them to pay insults to everybody—his wife first and foremost.

The sisters were greatly mortified when they saw Beauty

dressed like a princess, and more beautiful than the dawn. Her caresses were ignored, and the jealousy which they could not stifle only grew worse when she told them how happy she was. Out into the garden went the envious pair, there to vent their spleen to the full.

"Why should this chit be happier than we are?" each demanded of the other; "are we not much nicer than she is?"

"Sister," said the elder, "I have an idea. Let us try to persuade her to stay here longer than the eight days. Her stupid Beast will fly into a rage when he finds she has broken her word, and will very likely devour her."

"You are right, sister," said the other; "but we must make a great fuss of her if we are to make the plan successful."

With this plot decided upon they went upstairs again, and paid such attention to their little sister that Beauty wept for joy. When the eight days had passed the two sisters tore their hair, and showed such grief over her departure that she promised to remain another eight days.

Beauty reproached herself, nevertheless, with the grief she was causing to the poor Beast; moreover, she greatly missed not seeing him. On the tenth night of her stay in her father's house she dreamed that she was in the palace garden, where she saw the Beast lying on the grass nearly dead, and that he upbraided her for her ingratitude. Beauty woke up with a start, and burst into tears.

"I am indeed very wicked," she said, "to cause so much grief to a Beast who has shown me nothing but kindness. Is it his fault that he is so ugly, and has so few wits? He is good, and that makes up for all the rest. Why did I not wish to marry him? I should have been a good deal happier with him than my sisters are with their husbands. It is neither good looks nor brains in a husband that make a woman happy; it is beauty of character, virtue, kindness. All these qualities the Beast has. I admit I have no love for him, but he has my esteem, friendship, and gratitude. At all events I must not make him miserable, or I shall reproach myself all my life."

With these words Beauty rose and placed her ring on the table.

Hardly had she returned to her bed than she was asleep, and when she woke the next morning she saw with joy that she was in the Beast's palace. She dressed in her very best on purpose to please him, and nearly died of impatience all day, waiting for nine o'clock in the evening. But the clock struck in vain: no Beast appeared. Beauty now thought she must have caused his death, and rushed about the palace with loud despairing cries. She looked everywhere, and at last, recalling her dream, dashed into the garden by the canal, where she had seen him in her sleep. There she found the poor Beast lying unconscious, and thought he must be dead. She threw herself on his body, all her horror of his looks forgotten, and, feeling his heart still beat, fetched water from the canal and threw it on his face.

The Beast opened his eyes and said to Beauty:

"You forgot your promise. The grief I felt at having lost you made me resolve to die of hunger; but I die content since I have the pleasure of seeing you once more."

"Dear Beast, you shall not die," said Beauty; "you shall live and become my husband. Here and now I offer you my hand, and swear that I will marry none but you. Alas, I fancied I felt only friendship for you, but the sorrow I have experienced clearly proves to me that I cannot live without you."

Beauty had scarce uttered these words when the castle became ablaze with lights before her eyes: fireworks, music—all proclaimed a feast. But these splendours were lost on her: she turned to her dear Beast, still trembling for his danger.

Judge of her surprise now! At her feet she saw no longer the Beast, who had disappeared, but a prince, more beautiful than Love himself, who thanked her for having put an end to his enchantment. With good reason were her eyes riveted upon the prince, but she asked him nevertheless where the Beast had gone.

"You see him at your feet," answered the prince. "A wicked fairy condemned me to retain that form until some beautiful girl should consent to marry me, and she forbade me to betray any sign of intelligence. You alone in all the world could show yourself susceptible to the kindness of my character, and in offering you my crown I do but discharge the obligation that I owe you."

In agreeable surprise Beauty offered her hand to the handsome prince, and assisted him to rise. Together they repaired to the castle, and Beauty was overcome with joy to find, assembled in the hall, her father and her entire family. The lady who had appeared to her in her dream had had them transported to the castle.

"Beauty," said this lady (who was a celebrated fairy), "come and receive the reward of your noble choice. You preferred merit to either beauty or wit, and you certainly deserve to find these qualities combined in one person. It is your destiny to become a great queen, but I hope that the pomp of royalty will not destroy your virtues. As for you, ladies," she continued, turning to Beauty's two sisters, "I know your hearts and the malice they harbour. Your doom is to become statues, and under the stone that wraps you round to retain all your feelings. You will stand at the door of your sister's palace, and I can visit no greater punishment upon you than that you shall be witnesses of her happiness. Only when you recognise your faults can you return to your present shape, and I am very much afraid that you will be statues for ever. Pride, ill-temper, greed, and laziness can all be corrected, but nothing short of a miracle will turn a wicked and envious heart."

In a trice, with a tap of her hand, the fairy transported them all to the prince's realm, where his subjects were delighted to see him again. He married Beauty, and they lived together for a long time in happiness the more perfect because it was founded on virtue.

Your doom is to become statues

THE FRIENDLY FROG

ONCE upon a time there was a king who had been at war for a long time with his neighbours. After many battles had been fought his capital was besieged by the enemy. Fearing for the safety of the queen, the king implored her to take refuge in a stronghold to which he himself had never been but once. The queen besought him with tears to let her remain at his side, and share his fate, and lamented loudly when the king placed her in the carriage which was to take her away under escort.

The king promised to slip away whenever possible and pay her a visit, seeking thus to comfort her, although he knew that there was small chance of the hope being fulfilled. For the castle was a long way off, in the midst of a dense forest, and only those with a thorough knowledge of the roads could possibly reach it.

The queen was broken-hearted at having to leave her husband exposed to the perils of war, and though she made her journey by easy stages, lest the fatigue of so much travelling should make her ill, she was downcast and miserable when at length she reached the castle. She made excursions into the country round about, when sufficiently recovered, but found nothing to amuse or distract her. On all sides wide barren spaces met her eye, melancholy rather than pleasant to look upon.

"How different from my old home!" she exclaimed, as she gloomily surveyed the scene; "if I stay here long I shall die. To whom can I talk in this solitude? To whom can I unburden my grief? What have I done that the king should exile me? He must wish me, I suppose, to feel the bitterness of separation to the utmost, since he banishes me to this hateful castle."

She grieved long and deeply, and though the king wrote every day to her with good news of the way the siege was going, she became more and more unhappy. At last she determined that she would go back to him, but knowing that her attendants had been forbidden to let her return, except under special orders from the king, she kept her intention to herself. On the pretext of wishing sometimes to join the hunt, she ordered a small chariot, capable of accommodating one person only, to be built for her. This she drove herself, and used to keep up with the hounds so closely that she would leave the rest of the hunt behind. The chariot being in her sole control, this gave her the opportunity to escape whenever she liked, and the only obstacle was her lack of familiarity with the roads through the forest. She trusted, however, to the favour of Providence to bring her safely through it.

She now gave orders for a great hunt to be held, and intimated her wish that every one should attend. She herself was to be present in her chariot, and she proposed that every follower of the chase should choose a different line, and so close every avenue of escape to the quarry. The arrangements were carried out according to the queen's plan. Confident that she would soon see her husband again, she donned her most becoming attire. Her hat was trimmed with feathers of different colours, the front of her dress with a number of precious stones. Thus adorned, she looked in her beauty (which was of no ordinary stamp) like a second Diana.

When the excitement of the chase was at its height she gave

rein to her horses, urging them on with voice and whip, until their pace quickened to a gallop. But then, getting their bits between their teeth, the team sped onwards so fast that presently the chariot seemed to be borne upon the wind, and to be travelling faster than the eye could follow. Too late the poor queen repented of her rashness. "What possessed me," she cried, "to think that I could manage such wild and fiery steeds? Alack! What will become of me! What would the king do if he knew of my great peril? He only sent me away because he loves me dearly, and wished me to be in greater safety—and this is the way I repay his tender care!"

Her piteous cries rang out upon the air, but though she called on Heaven and invoked the fairies to her aid, it seemed that all the unseen powers had forsaken her.

Over went the chariot. She lacked the strength to jump clear quickly enough, and her foot was caught between the wheel and the axle-tree. It was only by a miracle that she was not killed, and she lay stretched on the ground at the foot of a tree, with her heart scarcely beating and her face covered with blood, unable to speak.

For a long time she lay thus. At last she opened her eyes and saw, standing beside her, a woman of gigantic stature. The latter wore nought but a lion's skin; her arms and legs were bare, and her hair was tied up with a dried snake's skin, the head of which dangled over her shoulder. In her hand she carried, for walking-stick, a stone club, and a quiver full of arrows hung at her side.

This extraordinary apparition convinced the queen that she was dead, and indeed it seemed impossible that she could have survived so terrible a disaster. "No wonder death needs resolution," she murmured, "since sights so terrible await one in the other world."

The Friendly Frog

The giantess overheard these words, and laughed to find the queen thought herself dead.

"Courage," she said; "you are still in the land of the living, though your lot is not improved. I am the Lion-Witch. My dwelling is near by; you must come and live with me."

"If you will have the kindness, good Lion-Witch, to take me back to my castle, the king, who loves me dearly, will not refuse you any ransom you demand, though it were the half of his kingdom."

"I will not do that," replied the giantess, "for I have wealth enough already. Moreover, I am tired of living alone, and as you have your wits about you it is possible you may be able to amuse me."

With these words she assumed the shape of a lioness, and taking the queen on her back, bore her off into the depths of a cavern. There she anointed the queen's wounds with an essence which quickly healed them.

But imagine the wonder and despair of the queen to find herself in this dismal lair! The approach to it was by ten thousand steps, which led downward to the centre of the earth, and the only light was that which came from a number of lofty lamps, reflected in a lake of quicksilver. This lake teemed with monsters, each of which was hideous enough to have terrified one far less timid than the queen. Ravens, screech-owls, and many another bird of evil omen filled the air with harsh cries. Far off could be espied a mountain, from the slopes of which there flowed the tears of all hapless lovers. Its sluggish stream was fed by every ill-starred love. The trees had neither leaves nor fruit, and the ground was cumbered with briars, nettles, and rank weeds. The food, too, was such as might be expected in such a horrid clime. A few dried roots, horsechestnuts, and thorn-apples—this was all the fare with which the Lion-Witch appeased the hunger of those who fell into her clutches.

When the queen was well enough to be set to work, the Witch told her she might build herself a hut, since she was fated to remain in her company for the rest of her life. On hearing this the queen burst into tears. "Alas!" she cried, "what have I done that you should keep me here? If my death, which I feel to be nigh, will cause you any pleasure, then I implore you to kill me: I dare not hope for any other kindness from you. But do not condemn me to the sadness of a life-long separation from my husband."

But the Lion-Witch merely laughed at her, bidding her dry her tears, if she would be wise, and do her part to please her. Otherwise, she declared, her lot would be the most miserable in the world.

"And what must I do to soften your heart?" replied the queen.

"I have a liking for fly-pastries," said the Lion-Witch; "and you must contrive to catch flies enough to make me a large and tasty one."

"But there are no flies here," rejoined the queen; "and even if there were there is not enough light to catch them by. Moreover, supposing I caught some, I have never in my life made pastry. You are therefore giving me orders which I cannot possibly carry out."

"No matter," said the pitiless Lion-Witch; "what I want I will have!"

The queen made no reply, but reflected that, no matter how cruel the Witch might be, she had only one life to lose, and in her present plight what terror could death hold for her? She did not attempt to look for flies, therefore, but sat down beneath a yew tree, and gave way to tears and lamentations. "Alas, dear husband," she cried, "how grieved you will be when you go to fetch me from the castle, and find me gone! You will suppose me to be dead or faithless; how I hope that you will mourn the loss of my life, not the loss of my love! Perhaps the remains of my chariot will be found in the wood, with all the ornaments I had put on to please you: at sight of these you will not doubt any more that I am dead. But then, how do I know that you will not bestow on some one else the heartfelt love which once belonged to me? At all events I shall be spared the sorrow of that knowledge, since I am never to return to the world."

These thoughts would have filled her mind for a long time, but she was interrupted by the dismal croaking of a raven overhead. Lifting her eyes, she saw in the dim light a large raven on the point of swallowing a frog which it held in its beak. "Though I have no hope of help for myself," she said, "I will not let this unfortunate frog die, if I can save it; though our lots are so different, its sufferings are quite as great as mine." She picked up the first stick which came to hand, and made the raven let go its prey. The frog fell to the ground and lay for a time half stunned; but as soon as it could think, in its froggish way, it began to speak. "Beautiful queen," it said, "you are the first friendly soul that I have seen since my curiosity brought me here."

"By what magic are you endowed with speech, little Frog?" replied the queen; "and what people are they whom you see here? I have seen none at all as yet."

"All the monsters with which the lake is teeming," replied the little Frog, "were once upon a time in the world. Some sat on

The approach to it was by ten thousand steps

The Friendly Frog

thrones, some held high positions at Court; there are even some royal ladies here who were the cause of strife and bloodshed. It is these latter whom you see in the shape of leeches, and

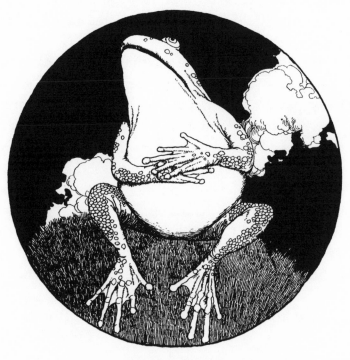

The Friendly Frog

they are condemned to remain here for a certain time. But of those who come here none ever returns to the world better or wiser."

"I can quite understand," said the queen, "that wicked people are not improved by merely being thrown together. But how is it that you are here, my friendly little Frog?"

"I came here out of curiosity," she replied. "I am part fairy, and though, in certain directions, my powers are limited, in others they are far-reaching. The Lion-Witch would kill me if she knew that I was in her domain."

"Whatever your fairy powers," said the queen, "I cannot understand how you could have fallen into the raven's clutches and come so near to being devoured."

"That is easily explained," said the Frog. "I have nought to fear when my little cap of roses is on my head, for that is the source of my power. Unluckily I had left it in the marsh when that ugly raven pounced upon me, and but for you, Madam, I should not now be here. Since you have saved my life, you have only to command me and I will do everything in my power to lessen the misfortunes of your lot."

"Alas, dear Frog," said the queen, "the wicked fairy who holds me captive desires that I should make her a fly-pastry. But there are no flies here, and if there were I could not see to catch them in the dim light. I am like, therefore, to get a beating which will kill me."

"Leave that to me," said the Frog, "I will quickly get you some."

Thereupon the Frog smeared sugar all over herself, and the same was done by more than six thousand of her froggy friends. They then made for a place where the fairy had a large store of flies, which she used to torment some of her luckless victims. No sooner did the flies smell the sugar than they flew to it, and found themselves sticking to the frogs. Away, then, went the latter at a gallop, to bring their friendly aid to the queen. Never was there such a catching of flies before, nor a better pastry than the one the queen made for the fairy. The surprise of the Witch was great

The Friendly Frog

when the queen handed it to her, for she was baffled to think how the flies could have been so cleverly caught.

The queen suffered so much from want of protection against the poisonous air that she cut down some cypress branches and began to build herself a hut. The Frog kindly offered her services. She summoned round her all those who had helped in the fly hunt, and they assisted the queen to build as pretty a little place to live in as you could find anywhere in the world.

But no sooner had she lain down to rest than the monsters of the lake, envious of her repose, gathered round the hut. They set up the most hideous noise that had ever been heard, and drove her so nearly mad that she got up and fled in fear and trembling from the house. This was just what the monsters were after, and a dragon, who had once upon a time ruled tyrannously over one of the greatest countries of the world, immediately took possession of it.

The poor queen tried to protest against this ill-treatment. But no one would listen to her: the monsters laughed and jeered at her, and the Lion-Witch said that if she came and dinned lamentations into her ears again she would give her a sound thrashing.

The queen was therefore obliged to hold her tongue. She sought out the Frog, who was the most sympathetic creature in the world, and they wept together; for the moment she put on her cap of roses the Frog became able to laugh or weep like anybody else.

"I am so fond of you," said the Frog to the queen, "that I will build your house again, though every monster in the lake should be filled with envy."

Forthwith she cut some wood, and a little country mansion for the queen sprang up so quickly that she was able to sleep in it that very night. Nothing that could make for the queen's comfort was forgotten by the Frog, and there was even a bed of wild thyme.

When the wicked fairy learnt that the queen was not sleeping on the ground, she sent for her and asked:

"What power is it, human or divine, that protects you? This land drinks only a rain of burning sulphur, and has never produced so much as a sage-leaf: yet they tell me fragrant herbs spring up beneath your feet."

"I cannot explain it, madam," said the queen, "unless it is due to the child I am expecting. Perhaps for her a less unhappy fate than mine is in store."

"I have a craving just now," said the Witch, "for a posy of rare flowers. See if this happiness which you expect will enable you to get them. If you do not succeed, such a thrashing as I know well how to give is surely in store for you."

The queen began to weep, for threats like these distressed her, and she despaired as she thought of the impossibility of finding flowers. But when she returned to her little house, the friendly Frog met her.

"How unhappy you look!" she said.

"Alas, dear friend," said the queen, "who would not be so? The Witch has demanded a posy of the most beautiful flowers. Where am I to find them? You see what sort of flowers grow here! Yet my life is forfeit if I do not procure them."

"Dear queen," said the Frog tenderly, "we must do our best to extricate you from this dilemma. Hereabouts there lives a bat of my acquaintance—a kindly soul. She moves about more quickly than I do, so I will give her my cap of roses, and with the aid of this she will be able to find you flowers."

The Friendly Frog

The queen curtseyed low, it being quite impossible to embrace the Frog, and the latter went off at once to speak to the bat. In a few hours the bat came back with some exquisite flowers tucked under her wings. Off went the queen with them to the Witch, who was more astonished than ever, being quite unable to understand in what marvellous way the queen had been assisted.

The queen never ceased to plot some means of escape, and told the Frog of her longings. "Madam," said the latter, "allow me first to take counsel with my little cap, and we will make plans according to what it advises." Having placed her cap upon some straw, she burnt in front of it a few juniper twigs, some capers, and a couple of green peas. She then croaked five times. This completed the rites, and having donned her cap again, she began to speak like an oracle.

"Fate, the all-powerful, decrees that you must not leave this place. You will have a little princess more beautiful than Venus herself. Let nothing fret you; time alone can heal."

The queen bowed her head and shed tears, but she determined to have faith in the friend she had found. "Whatever happens," she said, "do not leave me here alone, and befriend me when my little one is born." The Frog promised to remain with her, and did her best to comfort her.

It is now time to return to the king. So long as the enemy kept him confined within his capital he could not regularly send messengers to the queen. But at length, after many sorties, he forced the enemy to raise the siege. This success gave him pleasure not so much on his own account, as for the sake of the queen, who could now be brought home in safety. He knew nothing of the disaster which had befallen her, for none of his retinue had dared to tell him of it. They had found in the forest the remains of the chariot, the runaway horses, and the apparel in which she had driven forth to find her husband, and being convinced that she was killed or devoured by wild beasts, their one idea was to make the king believe that she had died suddenly.

It seemed as if the king could not survive this mournful news. He tore his hair, wept bitterly, and lamented his loss with all manner of sorrowful cries and sobs and sighs. For several days he would see nobody, and hid himself from view. Later, he returned to his capital and entered upon a long period of mourning, to the sincerity of which his heartfelt sorrow bore even plainer testimony than his sombre garb of woe. His royal neighbours all sent ambassadors with messages of condolence, and when the ceremonies proper to these occasions were at length over, he proclaimed a period of peace. He released his subjects from military service, and devoted himself to giving them every assistance in the development of commerce.

Of all this the queen knew nothing. A little princess had been born to her in the meantime, and her beauty did not belie the Frog's prediction. They gave her the name of Moufette, but the queen had great difficulty in persuading the Witch to let her bring up the child, for her ferocity was such that she would have liked to kill it.

At the age of six months Moufette was a marvel of beauty, and often, as she gazed upon her with mingled tenderness and pity, the queen would say:

"Could your father but see you, my poor child, how delighted he would be, and how dear you would be to him! But perhaps even now he has begun to forget me: doubtless he believes that death has robbed him of us, and it may be that another now fills the place I had in his affections."

Many were the tears she shed over these sad thoughts, and the Frog, whose love for her was sincere, was moved one day by the sight of her grief to say to her:

"If you like, Madam, I will go and seek your royal husband. It is a long journey, and I am but a tardy traveller, but sooner or later I have no doubt I shall get there."

No suggestion could have been more warmly approved, the queen clasping her hands, and bidding little Moufette do the same, in token of the gratitude she felt towards the good Frog for offering to make the expedition. Nor would the king, she declared, be less grateful. "Of what advantage, however," she went on, "will it be to him to learn that I am in this dire abode, since it will be impossible for him to rescue me from it?"

"That we must leave to Providence, Madam," said the Frog; "we can but make those efforts of which we are capable."

They took farewell of each other, and the queen sent a message to the king. This was written with her blood on a piece of rag, for she had neither ink nor paper. The good Frog was bringing him news of herself, she wrote, and she implored him to give heed to all that she might tell him, and to believe everything she had to say.

It took the Frog a year and four days to climb the ten thousand steps which led from the gloomy realm in which she had left the queen, up into the world. Another year was spent in preparing her equipage, for she was too proud to consent to appear at Court like a poor and humble frog from the marshes. A little sedan-chair was made for her, large enough to hold a couple of eggs comfortably, and this was covered outside with tortoise-shell and lined with lizardskin. From the little green frogs that hop about the meadows she selected fifty to act as maids of honour, and each of these was mounted on a snail. They had dainty saddles, and rode in dashing style with the leg thrown over the saddle-bow. A numerous bodyguard of rats, dressed like pages, ran before the snails—in short, nothing so captivating had ever been seen before. To crown all, the cap of roses, which never faded but was always in full bloom, most admirably became her. Being something of a coquette, too, she could not refrain from a touch of rouge and a patch or two; indeed, some said she was painted like a great many other ladies of the land, but it has been proved by inquiry that this report had its origin with her enemies.

The journey lasted seven years, and during all that time the poor queen endured unutterable pain and suffering. Had it not been for the solace of the beautiful Moufette she must have died a hundred times. Every word that the dear little creature uttered filled her with delight; indeed, with the exception of the Lion-Witch, there was nobody who was not charmed by her.

There came at length a day, after the queen had lived for six years in this dismal region, when the Witch told her that she could go hunting with her, on condition that she yielded up everything which she killed. The queen's joy when she once more saw the sun may be imagined; though at first she thought she would be blinded, so unaccustomed to its light had she become. So quick and lively was Moufette, even at five or six years of age, that she never failed in her aim, and mother and daughter together were thus able to appease somewhat the fierce instincts of the Witch.

Meanwhile the Frog was travelling over hills and valleys. Day or night, she never stopped, and at last she came nigh to the capital, where the king was now in residence. To her astonishment signs of festivity met her eye at every turn; on all sides there was merriment, song and dancing, and the nearer she came to the city the more festive seemed the mood of the people. All flocked with amazement to see her rustic retinue, and by the time she reached the city the crowd had become so large that it was with difficulty she made her way to the palace.

At the palace all was splendour, for the king, who had been deprived of his wife's society for nine years, had at last yielded to the petitions of his subjects, and was about to wed a princess who possessed many amiable qualities, though she lacked, admittedly, the beauty of his wife.

The good Frog descended from her sedan-chair, and with her attendants in her train entered the royal presence. To request an audience was unnecessary, for the king and his intended bride and all the princes were much too curious to learn why she had come to think of interrupting her.

"Sire," said the Frog, "I am in doubt whether the news I bring will cause you joy or sorrow. I can only conclude, from the marriage which you are proposing to celebrate, that you are no longer faithful to your queen."

Tears fell from the king's eyes. "Her memory is as dear to me as ever," he declared; "but you must know, good Frog, that monarchs cannot always follow their own wishes. For nine years now my subjects have been urging me to take a wife, and indeed it is due to them that there should be an heir to the throne. Hence my choice of this young princess, whose charms are apparent."

"I warn you not to marry her," rejoined the Frog; "the queen is not dead, and I am the bearer of a letter from her, writ in her own blood. There has been born to you a little daughter, Moufette, who is more beautiful than the very heavens."

The king took the rag on which the short message from the queen was written. He kissed it and moistened it with his tears; and declared, holding it up for all to see, that he recognised the handwriting of his wife. Then he plied the Frog with endless questions, to all of which she replied with lively intelligence.

The princess who was to have been queen, and the envoys who were attending the marriage ceremony, were somewhat out of countenance. "Sire," said one of the most distinguished guests, turning to the king, "can you contemplate the breaking of your solemn pledge upon the word of a toad like that? This scum of the marshes has the audacity to come and lie to the entire Court, just for the gratification of being listened to!"

"I would have you know, your Excellency," replied the Frog, "that I am no scum of the marshes. Since you force me to display my powers—hither, fairies all!"

At these words the frogs, the rats, the snails, and the lizards all suddenly ranged themselves behind the Frog. But in place of their familiar natural forms, they appeared now as tall, majestic figures, handsome of mien, and with eyes that outshone the stars. Each wore a crown of jewels on his head, while over his shoulders hung a royal mantle of velvet, lined with ermine, the train of which was borne by dwarfs. Simultaneously the sound of trumpets, drums, and hautboys filled the air with martial melody, and all the fairies began to dance a ballet, with step so light that the least spring lifted them to the vaulted ceiling of the chamber.

The astonishment of the king and his future bride was in no

The journey lasted seven years

The Friendly Frog

way diminished when the fairy dancers suddenly changed before their eyes into flowers—jasmine, jonquils, violets, roses, and carnations—which carried on the dance just as though they were possessed of legs and feet. It was as though a flower-bed had come to life, every movement of which gave pleasure alike to eye and nostril. A moment later the flowers vanished, and in their place were fountains of leaping water that fell in a cascade and formed a lake beneath the castle walls. On the surface of the lake were little boats, painted and gilt, so pretty and dainty that the princess challenged the ambassadors to a voyage. None hesitated to do so, for they thought it was all a gay pastime, and a merry prelude to the marriage festivities. But no sooner had they embarked than boats, fountains, and lake vanished, and the frogs were frogs once more.

"Sire," said the Frog, when the king asked what had become of the princess, "your wife alone is your queen. Were my affection for her less than it is, I should not interfere; but she deserves so well, and your daughter Moufette is so charming, that you ought not to lose one moment in setting out to their rescue."

"I do assure you, Madam Frog," replied the king, "that if I could believe my wife to be alive, I would shrink from nothing in the world for sight of her again."

"Surely," said the Frog, "after the marvels I have shown you, there ought not to be doubt in your mind of the truth of what I say. Leave your realm in the hands of those whom you can trust, and set forth without delay. Take this ring—it will provide you with the means of seeing the queen, and of speaking with the Lion-Witch, notwithstanding that she is the most formidable creature in the world."

The king refused to let any one accompany him, and after

The Friendly Frog

bestowing handsome gifts upon the Frog, he set forth. "Do not lose heart," she said to him; "you will encounter terrible difficulties, but I am convinced that your desires will meet with success." He plucked up courage at these words, and started upon the quest of his dear wife, though he had only the ring to guide him.

Now Moufette's beauty became more and more perfect as she grew older, and all the monsters of the lake of quicksilver were enamoured of her. Hideous and terrifying to behold, they came and lay at her feet. Although Moufette had seen them ever since she was born, her lovely eyes could never grow accustomed to them, and she would run away and hide in her mother's arms. "Shall we remain here long?" she would ask; "are we never to escape from misery?"

The queen would answer hopefully, so as to keep up the spirits of the child, but in her heart hope had died. The absence of the Frog and the lack of any news from her, together with the long time that had passed since she had heard anything of the king, filled her with grief and despair.

By now it had become a regular thing for them to go hunting with the Lion-Witch. The latter liked good things, and enjoyed the game which they killed for her. The head or the feet of the quarry was all the share they got, but there was compensation in being allowed to look again upon the daylight. The Witch would take the shape of a lioness, and the queen and her daughter would seat themselves on her back. In this fashion they ranged the forests a-hunting.

One day, when the king was resting in a forest to which his ring had guided him, he saw them shoot by like an arrow from the bow. They did not perceive him, and when he tried to follow them he lost sight of them completely. The queen was still as beautiful as of old, despite all that she had suffered, and she seemed to her husband more attractive than ever, so that he longed to have her with him again. He felt certain that the young princess with her was his dear little Moufette, and he resolved to face death a thousand times rather than abandon his intention of rescuing her.

With the assistance of his ring he penetrated to the gloomy region in which the queen had been for so many years. His astonishment was great to find himself descending to the centre of the earth, but with every new thing that met his eyes his amazement grew greater.

The Lion-Witch, from whom nothing was hid, knew well the day and hour of his destined arrival. Much did she wish that the powers in league with her could have ordered things otherwise, but she resolved to pit her strength against his to the full.

She built a palace of crystal which floated in the midst of the lake of quicksilver, rising and falling on its waves. Therein she imprisoned the queen and her daughter, and assembling the monsters, who were all admirers of Moufette, she gave them this warning:

"You will lose this beautiful princess if you do not help me to keep her from a gallant who has come to bear her away."

The monsters vowed that they would do everything in their power, and forthwith they surrounded the palace of crystal. The less heavy stationed themselves upon the roofs and walls, others mounted guard at the doors, while the remainder filled the lake.

Following the dictates of his faithful ring, the king went first to the Witch's cavern. She was waiting for him in the form of a lioness, and the moment he appeared she sprang upon him. But she was not prepared for his valiant swordsmanship, and as she put forth a paw to fell him to the ground, he cut it off at the elbow-joint. She yelped loudly and fell over, whereupon he went up to her and set his foot upon her throat, swearing that he would kill her. Notwithstanding her uncontrollable rage, and the fact that she had nothing to fear from wounds, she felt cowed by him.

"What do you seek to do to me?" she asked; "what do you want of me?"

"I intend to punish you," replied the king with dignity, "for having carried away my wife. Deliver her up to me, or I will strangle you on the spot."

"Turn your eyes to the lake," she answered, "and see if it lies in my power to do so."

The king followed the direction she indicated, and saw the queen and her daughter in the palace of crystal, where it floated like a boat without oars or rudder on the lake of quicksilver. He was like to die of mingled joy and sorrow. He shouted to them at the top of his voice, and they heard him. But how was he to reach them?

While he pondered a plan for the accomplishment of this, the Lion-Witch vanished. He ran round and round the lake, but no sooner did the palace draw near enough, at one point or another, to let him make a spring for it, than it suddenly receded with menacing speed. As often as his hopes were raised they were dashed to the ground.

Fearing that he would presently tire, the queen cried to him that he must not lose courage, for the Lion-Witch sought to wear him down, but that true love could brave all obstacles. She stretched out imploring hands, and so did Moufette. At sight of

The Friendly Frog

this the king felt his courage renewed within him. Lifting his voice, he declared that he would rather live the rest of his life in this dismal region than go away without them.

Patience he certainly needed, for no monarch in the world ever spent such a miserable time. There was only the ground, cumbered with briars and thorns, for bed, and for food he had only wild fruit more bitter than gall. In addition, he was under the perpetual necessity of defending himself from the monsters of the lake.

Three years went by in this fashion, and the king could not pretend that he had gained the least advantage. He was almost in despair, and many a time was tempted to cast himself into the lake. He would have done so without hesitation had there been any hope that thereby the sufferings of the queen and the princess could be alleviated.

One day as he was running, after his custom, from one side of the lake to the other, he was hailed by one of the ugliest of the dragons. "Swear by your crown and sceptre, by your kingly robe, by your wife and child," said the monster, "to give me a certain tit-bit to eat for which I have a fancy, whenever I shall ask for it, and I will take you on my back: none of the monsters in this lake which are guarding the palace will prevent us from carrying away the queen and Princess Moufette."

"Best of dragons!" cried the king; "I swear to you, and to all of dragon blood, that you shall have your fill of whatsoever you desire, and I will be for ever your devoted servant."

"Promise nothing which you do not mean to fulfill," replied the dragon; "for otherwise life-long misfortunes may overwhelm you."

The Friendly Frog

The king repeated his assurances, for he was dying of impatience to regain his beloved queen, and mounted the dragon just as though he were the most dashing of steeds. But now the other monsters rushed to bar the way. The combat was joined, and nought was audible save the hissing of the serpents, nought visible save the brimstone, fire and sulphur, which were belched forth in every direction.

The king reached the palace at last, but there fresh efforts were required of him, for the entrances were defended by bats and owls and ravens. But even the boldest of these was torn to pieces by the dragon, who attacked them tooth and nail. The queen, too, who was a spectator of this savage fight, kicked down chunks of the wall, and armed with these helped her dear husband in the fray. Victory at length rested with them, and as they flew to one another's arms, the enchantment was brought to an end by a thunderbolt which plunged into the lake and dried it up.

The friendly dragon vanished, along with all the other monsters, and the king found himself (by what means he had not the least idea) home again in his own city, and seated, with his queen and Moufette beside him, in a splendid dining-hall before a table laid with the richest fare. Never before was there such amazement and delight as theirs. The populace came running for a sight of the queen and princess, and to add to the wonder of it all, the latter was seen to be attired in apparel of such magnificence that the gaze was almost dazzled by her jewels.

You can easily imagine what festivities now took place at the palace. There were masquerades, and tournaments with tilting at the ring which attracted the highest princes from all over the

The Friendly Frog

world; even more were these drawn by the bright eyes of Moufette.

Amongst the handsomest and most accomplished in skill-at-arms, there was none anywhere who could outshine Prince Moufy. He won the applause and admiration of all, and Moufette, who had hitherto known only dragons and serpents, was not backward in according him her share of praise. Prince Moufy was deeply in love with her, and not a day passed but he showed her some fresh attention in the hope of gaining her favour. In due course he offered himself as a suitor, informing the king and queen that his realm was of a richness and extent that might well claim their favourable consideration.

The king replied that Moufette should make her own choice of husband, for his only wish was to please her and make her happy. With this answer the prince was well satisfied, for he was already aware that the princess was not indifferent to him. He offered her his hand, and she declared that if he were not to be her husband, then no other man should be. Prince Moufy threw himself in rapture at her feet, and exacted, lover-like, a promise that she would keep her word with him.

The prince and princess were betrothed, and Prince Moufy then returned to his own realm, in order to make preparations for the marriage. Moufette wept much at his going, for she was oppressed by an inexplicable presentiment of evil. The prince likewise was much downcast, and the queen, noticing this, gave him a portrait of her daughter with an injunction to curtail the splendour of his preparations rather than allow his return to be delayed. The prince was nothing loth to obey her behest, and promised to adopt a course which so well consulted his own happiness.

The Friendly Frog

The princess amused herself with music during his absence, for in a few months she had learned to play exceedingly well.

One day, when she was in the queen's apartment, the king rushed in. Tears were streaming down his face as he took his daughter in his arms and cried aloud: "Alas, my child! O wretched father! O miserable king!" Sobs choked his utterance, and he could say no more.

Greatly alarmed, the queen and princess asked him what had happened, and at last he got out that there had just arrived an enormously tall giant, who professed to be an envoy of the dragon of the lake; and that in pursuance of the promise which the king had given in exchange for assistance in fighting the monsters, the dragon demanded that he should give up the princess, as he desired to make her into a pie for dinner. The king added that he had bound himself by solemn oaths to give the dragon what he asked —and in the days of which we are telling no one ever broke his word.

The queen received this dire news with piercing shrieks, and clasped her child to her bosom. "My life shall be forfeit," she cried, "ere my daughter is delivered up to this monster. Let him rather take our kingdom and all that we have. Unnatural father! Is it possible you can consent to such cruelty? What! My child to be made into a pie! The bare notion is intolerable! Send this grim envoy to me; it may be the spectacle of my anguish will soften his heart."

The king said nothing, but went in quest of the giant. He brought him to the queen, who flung herself at his feet with her daughter. She begged him to have mercy, and to persuade the dragon to take all that they possessed, but to spare Moufette's life.

The Friendly Frog

The giant replied, however, that the matter did not rest with him. The dragon, he said, was so obstinate, and so addicted to the pleasures of the table, that no power on earth would restrain him from eating what he had a mind to make a meal of. Furthermore, he counselled them, as a friend, to yield with a good grace lest greater ills should be in store. At these words the queen fainted, and the princess would have been in similar case, if she had not been obliged to go to the assistance of her mother.

No sooner was the dreadful news known throughout the palace than it spread all over the city. On all sides there was weeping and wailing, for Moufette was greatly beloved.

The king could not bring himself to give her up to the giant, and the latter, after waiting several days, grew restive and began to utter terrible threats. But the king and queen, taking counsel together, were agreed. "What is there worse that could happen to us?" they said; "if the dragon of the lake were to come and eat us all up, we could not suffer more, for if Moufette is put into a pie that will be the end of us."

Presently the giant informed them that he had received a message from the dragon, to the effect that if the princess would agree to marry one of his nephews, he would spare her life. This nephew was not only young and handsome, but a prince to boot; and there was no doubt of her being able to live very happily with him.

This proposal somewhat assuaged their grief, but when the queen mentioned it to the princess, she found her more ready to face death than entertain this marriage. "I cannot break faith just to save my life," said Moufette; "you promised me to Prince Moufy, and I will marry none else. Let me perish, for my death will enable you to live in peace." The king in his turn tried, with many endearments, to persuade her, but she could not be moved. Finally, therefore, it was arranged that she should be conducted to a mountaintop, there to await the dragon.

Everything was made ready for the great sacrificial rite, and nothing so mournful had ever been seen before. Black garments and pale, distraught faces were encountered at every turn. Four hundred maidens of the noblest birth, clad in long white robes and wearing crowns of cypress, accompanied the princess. The latter was borne in an open litter of black velvet, that all men might behold the wondrous miracle of her beauty. Her tresses, tied with crape, hung over her shoulders, and she wore a crown of jasmine and marigolds. The only thing that seemed to affect her was the grief of the king and queen, who walked behind her, overwhelmed with the burden of their sorrow. Beside the litter strode the giant, armed from top to toe, and looking hungrily at the princess, as though already he savoured his share of the dish she was to make. The air was filled with sighs and sobs, and the tears of the spectators made rivulets along the road.

"O Frog, dear Frog," cried the queen; "you have indeed forsaken me! Why give me help in that dismal place and refuse it to me here? Had I but died then, I should not now be mourning the end of all my hopes, and I should have been spared the agony of waiting to see my darling Moufette devoured."

Slowly the procession made its way to the summit of the fatal mountain. On arrival there the cries and lamentations broke out with renewed force, and a more pitiful noise was never heard before. The giant then directed that all farewells must be said, and a general withdrawal made, and his order was obeyed. Folks in

They reached the house where the light was burning
Page 186

I know you well, queen, and I know how frightened you are
Page 202

those days were docile and obedient, and never thought of combating ill-fortune.

The king and queen, with all the Court, now climbed another hill-top, from which they could obtain a view of all that happened to the princess. They had not long to wait, for they quickly espied a dragon, half a league long, sailing through the sky. He flew laboriously, for his bulk was so great that even six large wings could hardly support it. His body was covered all over with immense blue scales and tongues of poison flame, his twisted tail had fifty coils and another half coil beyond that, while his claws were each as big as a windmill. His jaws were agape, and inside could be seen three rows of teeth as long as an elephant's tusks.

Now while the dragon was slowly wending his way to the mountain-top, the good and faithful Frog, mounted on a hawk's back, was flying at full speed to Prince Moufy. She was wearing her cap of roses, and though he was locked in his privy chamber she needed no key to enter.

"Hapless lover!" she cried; "what are you doing here? This very moment, while you sit dreaming about her beauty, Moufette is in direst peril! See, here is a roseleaf; I have but to blow upon it and it will become a mettlesome steed."

As she spoke there suddenly appeared a green horse. It had twelve hoofs and three heads, and from the latter it could spit forth fire, bomb-shells, and cannon-balls respectively. The Frog then gave the prince a sword, eight yards long and no heavier than a feather, and a garment fashioned out of a single diamond. This he slipped on like a coat, and though it was hard as rock it was so pliant that his movements were in no way impeded.

"Now fly to the rescue of your love," said the Frog; "the

green horse will carry you to her. Do not omit to let her know, when you have delivered her, of what my part has been."

"Great-hearted fairy!" cried the prince, "this is no moment to return you thanks, but from henceforth I am your faithful servant."

Off went the horse with the three heads, galloping on its twelve hoofs three times as fast, and more, than the best of ordinary steeds; and in a very short time the prince had reached the mountain, where he found his dear princess all alone.

As the dragon slowly drew near, the green horse began to throw out fire, bomb-shells, and cannon-balls, which greatly disconcerted the monster. Twenty balls lodged in his throat, his scaly armour was dinted, and the bomb-shells put out one of his eyes. This enraged him, and he tried to hurl himself upon the prince. But the latter's long sword was so finely tempered that he could do what he liked with it, and now he plunged it in up to the hilt, now cut with it as though it had been a whip. The prince would have suffered, however, from the dragon's claws had it not been for his diamond coat, which was impenetrable.

Moufette had recognised her lover from afar, for the gleaming diamond which covered him was transparent; and she was like to die of terror at the risk he ran. The king and queen, however, felt hope revive within them. They had little thought to see arriving so opportunely a horse with three heads and twelve hoofs that breathed forth fire and flame, nor yet a prince, in diamond mail, and armed with so redoubtable a sword, who performed such prodigies of valour. The king put his hat on the end of his stick, the queen tied a handkerchief to hers, and with all the Court following suit, there was no lack of signals of encouragement to the prince. Not that such were necessary, for his own stout heart and the peril in which he saw Moufette were enough to keep his courage up.

Heavens, how he fought! Barbs, talons, horns, wings, and scales fell from the dragon till the ground was covered with them, and the soil was dyed blue and green with the mingled blood of dragon and horse. Five times the prince was unhorsed, but each time he picked himself up and composedly mounted his steed again. Then would follow such cannonades, bombardments, and flame-throwing as had never been seen or heard of before.

At length, its strength exhausted, the dragon fell, and the prince delivered a finishing stroke. None could believe their eyes when from the gaping wound so made there stepped forth a handsome and elegant prince, clad in a coat of blue and gold velvet, embroidered with pearls, and wearing on his head a little Grecian helmet with a crest of white feathers. With outstretched hands this new-comer ran to Prince Moufy and embraced him.

"How can I ever repay you, my gallant deliverer?" he cried. "Never was monarch confined in a more dreadful prison than the one from which you have freed me. It is sixteen years since the Lion-Witch condemned me to it, and I have languished there ever since. Moreover, such is her power that she would have obliged me, against my will, to devour that sweet princess. I beg you to let me pay my respects to her, and explain my hapless plight!"

Astonished and delighted by the remarkable way in which his adventure had ended, Prince Moufy lavished courtesies upon the newly-discovered prince. Together they went to Moufette, who rendered thanks a thousand times to Providence for her unexpected happiness. Already the king and queen and all the Court

The Friendly Frog

had joined her, and everybody spoke at once, and nobody listened to anybody, while nearly as many tears were shed for joy as a little time ago had been shed for grief. And finally, to set the crown on their rejoicing, the good Frog was espied flying through the air on her hawk. The latter had little golden bells upon its feet, and when the faint tinkling of these caused every one to look up, there was the Frog, beautiful as the dawn, with her cap of roses shining like the sun.

The queen ran to her and took her by one of her little paws. At that instant the wise Frog was transformed into a majestic royal lady of gracious mien. "I come," she cried, "to crown the faithful Moufette, who preferred to face death rather than break her word to Prince Moufy." With these words she placed two myrtle wreaths upon the lovers' heads; and at a signal of three taps from her wand the dragon's bones rose up and formed a triumphal arch to commemorate the auspicious occasion.

Back to the city went all the company, singing wedding songs as gladly as they had previously with sorrow bewailed the sacrifice of the princess. On the morrow the marriage took place, and with what festivities it was solemnised may be left to the imagination.

PRINCESS ROSETTE

O NCE upon a time there lived a king and queen who had
two handsome boys, and so well looked after were the
latter that they grew apace, like the daylight.

The queen never had a child without summoning the fairies to
be present at the birth, and she always begged them to tell what its
future was to be. When in due course she had a beautiful little
daughter—so pretty that one could not set eyes on her without
loving her—all the fairies came to visit her, and were hospitably
entertained. As they were making ready to go, the queen said to
them:

"Do not forget your friendly custom, but tell me what fortune
awaits Rosette." Such was the name which had been given to the
little princess.

The fairies replied that they had left their magic books at
home, but would come and see her some other time.

"Ah," said the queen, "that bodes ill. You are anxious not to
distress me by an unhappy prophecy. But tell me all, I implore
you, and hide nothing from me."

The fairies did their utmost to excuse themselves. But the
queen became more and more eager to learn everything, and at last
the chief of them made a declaration.

"We fear, Madam," she said, "that Rosette will bring disaster
on her brothers, and that in some fashion she will be the cause of

their death. This much and no more can we foretell of the pretty child, and we are grieved that we should have no better news to give you."

Then the fairies went away, and the queen was left grieving.

So deep was her grief that the king saw it in her face, and asked what ailed her. She had gone too near the fire, she told him, and had burnt all the flax that was on her distaff.

"Is that all?" said the king, and going up to his storeroom he brought her more flax than she could have spun in a hundred years.

But the queen continued sad, and again the king asked what ailed her. She declared that in walking by the river she had let her green satin slipper fall into the water.

"Is that all?" said the king, and summoning all the shoemakers in the kingdom he brought her ten thousand green satin slippers.

Still she grieved, and once more he asked what ailed her. She told him that in eating with rather too vigorous an appetite she had swallowed her wedding-ring, which had been on her finger. The king knew at once that she was not telling the truth, for he had put away this ring himself.

"My dear wife," he said, "you lie; I put away your ring in my purse—here it is!"

She was not a little confused at being caught telling a lie (for there is nothing in the world so ugly), and she saw that the king was displeased. She told him, therefore, what the fairies had prophesied of little Rosette, and implored him to say if he could think of any good remedy.

The king was plunged in the deepest melancholy, so much so that he remarked on one occasion to the queen: "I see no other means of saving our two sons but to bring about the death of our little child while she is still in long clothes." But the queen exclaimed that she would rather suffer death herself. She would never consent, she declared, to such a cruel course, and he must think of something else.

The royal pair were at their wits' end when the queen was told that in a forest near the city there lived an aged hermit. His habitation was a hollow tree, and folks were wont to seek his advice upon all manner of things. "I too must go there," said the queen; "the fairies have warned me of the evil, but they have forgotten to tell me of the remedy."

She rose betimes and mounted a dainty little white mule that was shod with gold, and took with her two of her ladies, each riding a bonny horse. When they had entered the wood they dismounted, as a sign of deference, and presented themselves at the tree where the hermit lived. The latter had an aversion from the sight of women, but on recognising the queen he addressed her.

"You are welcome," he said; "what do you want of me?"

She told him what the fairies had said of Rosette, and begged for advice. His reply was that the princess must be placed in a tower and never be allowed to leave it. The queen tendered her thanks, and having bestowed liberal alms upon him, returned to tell everything to the king.

When the king had heard her news he gave orders at once for a great tower to be built. In this the princess was shut up, and to keep her amused the king and queen and her two brothers went every day to see her. The elder boy was known as the Big Prince, and the younger as the Little Prince. Both were passionately attached to their sister, for she had such beauty and charm as had never been seen before. For the lightest of looks from her many would have paid a hundred gold pieces and more.

When the princess was fifteen years old the Big Prince spoke of her to his father. "My sister is old enough now to marry, Sire," he said; "shall we not soon be celebrating her wedding?" The Little Prince said the same thing to his mother. But their royal parents turned the conversation and made no answer on the subject of the marriage.

One day the king and queen were stricken by a grievous malady, and died almost within twenty-four hours. Throughout the realm there was mourning; every one wore black, and on all sides the tolling of bells was heard. Rosette was grieved beyond consolation by the death of her dear mother.

But when the royal dead had been interred, the noblemen of the realm set the Big Prince upon a throne of gold and diamonds, robed him in purple velvet embroidered with suns and moons, and placed a splendid crown upon his head. Then all the Court cried aloud three times: "Long live the King!" and there followed universal festivities and rejoicings.

"Now that we are in power," said the king and his brother as soon as they could converse in private, "we must release our sister from the tower in which she has languished so long." They had only to cross the garden to reach the tower, which was built in a corner. It had been reared as high as possible, for it had been the intention of the late king and queen that their daughter should remain in it for life.

Rosette was busy with embroidery when her brothers entered, but on catching sight of them she rose and left the frame at which she was working. Taking the king's hand, she said: "Good-morrow, Sire; you are king to-day, and I am your humble servant. I implore you to release me from the tower in which I have been languishing so long." And with these words she burst into tears.

The king embraced her and told her not to weep, for he had come to take her from the tower and establish her in a beautiful castle. The prince, who had brought a pocketful of sweets to give to Rosette, added his word. "Come," he said, "let us leave this hateful tower, and do not be unhappy any longer. Very soon the king will find a husband for you."

When Rosette saw the beautiful garden, with all its flowers and fruit and its many fountains, she was overcome with amazement and could not speak a word. She had never before seen anything of the kind. She looked about her on all sides, and then ran hither and thither, picking the fruit from the trees and the flowers from the beds, while her little dog Frillikin (who was as green as a parrot, had only one ear, and could dance deliciously) capered in front of her, yapping his loudest, and amusing everybody present by his absurd gambols.

Presently Frillikin dashed into a little copse, and the princess followed. Never was any one so struck with wonder as she, to behold there a great peacock with tail outspread. So beautiful, so exquisitely and perfectly beautiful did it seem to her that she could not take away her eyes. When the king and the prince joined her they asked what it was that had so taken her fancy. She pointed to the peacock and asked what it was, to which they replied that it was a bird that was sometimes served at table.

"What?" she cried; "a bird so beautiful as that to be killed and eaten? I tell you, I will marry no one but the King of the

Peacocks, and when I am queen no one shall ever eat such a dish again!"

No words can express the astonishment of the king. "My dear sister," he said, "where do you suppose that we are to find the King of the Peacocks?"

"Wherever you please, Sire," was the answer; "but I will marry none but him!"

After having announced this decision she allowed her brothers to escort her to their castle. But so great was the fancy she had taken to the peacock that she insisted on its being brought and placed in her apartment.

All the ladies of the Court, by whom Rosette had never yet been seen, now hastened to pay their dutiful respects. Gifts of every kind were proffered to her—sweetmeats and sugar, gay ribbons, and dresses of cloth-of-gold, dolls, slippers richly embroidered, with many pearls and diamonds. All did their best to show her attention, and she displayed such charming manners, kissing hands and curtseying so graciously when any gift was offered to her, that not a gentleman or lady of the Court but left her presence loud in her praise.

While the princess was being thus entertained, the king and the prince were taking counsel as to how they could find the King of the Peacocks, supposing such a person did really exist. In pursuit of the plan which they formed a portrait was painted of the Princess Rosette, and so cunningly wrought was this picture that only speech seemed wanting to make it live. Then they said to their sister:

"Since you will marry none but the King of the Peacocks, we are setting forth together in quest of him through the wide world.

Princess Rosette

Princess Rosette

If we find him we shall be well rewarded. Wait for our return, and take care of our kingdom while we are away."

Rosette thanked them for the trouble they were taking, and promised to govern the kingdom well. She declared that while they were away her only pleasures would be to admire the beautiful peacock and make Frillikin dance. Their adieux were said with many tears.

Behold, then, the royal pair upon their travels, asking of all whom they met: "Do you know the King of the Peacocks?" The reply from all was "No, we do not." Then the travellers would pass on and go further, journeying in this way so far, far away that no one had ever been so far before.

At last they reached the kingdom of the Cockchafers, and the latter in their myriads made so loud a buzzing that the king thought he would go deaf. He asked one who seemed more intelligent than the rest if he knew whereabouts the King of the Peacocks was to be found.

"Sire," said the cockchafer, "his kingdom is thirty thousand leagues away; you have taken the longest road to get there."

"How do you know that?" asked the king.

"Because we know you well," replied the cockchafer; "every year we spend two or three months in your garden!"

The king and his brother embraced the cockchafer warmly, and struck up a great friendship. Arm in arm they all went off to dinner, over which the visitors expressed their astonishment at the remarkable features of this country, where the smallest leaf from a tree was worth a gold piece. Presently they set off for their destination, and as they now knew the road they were not long in reaching it. They observed that all the trees were full of peacocks;

indeed the place held so many of them that their screaming as they talked could be heard two leagues away.

"If the King of the Peacocks is himself a peacock," said the king to his brother, "how can our sister dream of marrying him? It would be folly to sanction it. A nice set of relatives she would present to us—a lot of little peacocks for nephews!" The prince was equally uneasy in his mind. "It was an unfortunate notion to come into her head," he declared; "I cannot imagine how she ever came to think that such a person as the King of the Peacocks existed."

When they reached the city they found it peopled with men and women, but the latter all wore garments fashioned out of peacocks' feathers; and from the profusion in which these objects were everywhere to be seen it was plain that they were regarded with an intense admiration. They encountered the King of the Peacocks, who was out for a drive in a splendid little chariot of gold, studded with diamonds, drawn by a dozen galloping peacocks.

The King of the Peacocks, fair of complexion, with a crown of peacocks' feathers surmounting his long and curly yellow locks, was so extremely handsome that the king and prince were delighted with his appearance. He guessed from their clothes, so different from those of the natives, that they were strangers; but to make sure he caused his carriage to stop and summoned them to him.

The king and the prince advanced to meet him, and bowed low. "We have come from far away, Sire," they said, "in order to show you a portrait." With these words they drew from the pack which they carried the magnificent portrait of Rosette.

Princess Rosette

"I do not believe," said the King of the Peacocks, when he had looked long and well at it, "that the world holds so beautiful a maiden."

"She is a hundred times more beautiful than that," said the king.

"You are joking," said the King of the Peacocks.

"Sire," said the prince, "this is my brother, who is a monarch like yourself: men call him King. For myself, I am known as Prince. This portrait shows our sister, the Princess Rosette. We are here to ask if you are willing to marry her. She has good sense as well as good looks, and we will give her for dowry a bushel of golden crowns."

"Why, certainly," said the King of the Peacocks, "I will marry her with all my heart. I promise she shall want for nothing, and I will love her truly. But I would have you know that she must be as beautiful as her picture, and that if she falls short of it by the least little bit, you shall die."

"We accept the conditions," said Rosette's two brothers.

"You accept?" said the King of the Peacocks. "Then you must bide in prison until the princess has arrived."

The royal brothers raised no objection to this, for they knew well that Rosette was more beautiful than her portrait. The King of the Peacocks saw to it that his captives were well looked after, and went often to visit them. The portrait of Rosette was placed in his palace, and he was so taken up with it that, night or day, he could scarcely sleep.

From prison the king and the prince sent a letter to the princess telling her to pack at once all she might require and come as quickly as possible, for the King of the Peacocks awaited her. They did not dare to mention that they were in prison, lest she should be too uneasy.

When the princess received this letter her transports of delight were enough to kill her. She announced to every one that the King of the Peacocks had been found, and desired to wed her. Bonfires were lit, guns fired, and sugar and sweetmeats eaten in abundance; while for three days every one who came to see the princess was treated to bread and butter with jam, and cakes and ale.

Having dispensed hospitality in this liberal fashion, the princess gave all her beautiful dolls to her dearest friends, and entrusted her brother's realm to the wisest elders of the city. She bade them take care of everything, spend as little as possible, and save money until the king should return. At the same time she begged them to look after her peacock.

Taking with her only her nurse and foster-sister, and her little green dog Frillikin, she embarked on a vessel and put out to sea. They had with them the bushel of golden crowns, and clothes enough to last for ten years, with a change of dress twice a day; and they did nothing but laugh and sing on the voyage.

Presently the nurse said to the boatman:

"Tell me, tell me, are we near the Land of Peacocks?"

"Not yet, not yet," replied the boatman.

A little later she asked again:

"Tell me, tell me, are we near it now?"

"Presently, presently," replied the boatman.

Once more she asked:

"Tell me, tell me, are we near it now?"

"Very near, very near," said the boatman.

Princess Rosette

When he answered thus the nurse sat down beside him in the stern of the boat. "If you like, you can be rich for ever," she said to him.

The wicked nurse

"I should like that well," replied the boatman.

"If you like," she went on, "you can gain good money."

"I ask nothing better," said he.

"Very well, then," said the nurse; "to-night, when the princess is asleep, you must help me to throw her into the sea. When she is drowned I will dress up my daughter in her fine clothes, and we

Princess Rosette

will take her to the King of the Peacocks, who will be delighted to marry her. You shall have your fill of diamonds as reward."

The boatman was taken aback by this suggestion from the nurse. He declared it was a pity to drown so beautiful a princess, and that he had compassion for her. But the nurse fetched a bottle of wine, and plied him with drink until he no longer had wits enough left to refuse.

When night fell the princess went to sleep, according to her usual practice, with little Frillikin comfortably curled up at the foot of the bed, stirring not a paw. When Rosette was fast asleep the wicked nurse, who had remained awake, went to find the boatman. She took him to the cabin where the princess lay, and with the help of the foster-sister they lifted her up—feather-bed, mattress, sheets, blankets, and all—without disturbing her, and threw her into the sea just as she was. So soundly did the princess slumber that she never woke up.

Now luckily her bed was made of feathers from the phoenix, which are very rare and have this peculiar virtue that they never sink in water. Consequently the princess went floating along in her bed, just as though she were in a boat.

Presently, however, the water began little by little to lap first against the sides of the feather-bed, then against the mattress, until Rosette began to feel uncomfortable. She turned over restlessly, and Frillikin woke up. He had a very keen nose, and when he scented the soles and the cod-fish so near at hand he began yapping. He barked so loudly that he woke up all the other fish, and they began to swim round and about. Some of the big fish bumped their heads against the bed, and there being nothing to steady the latter it spun round and round like a top.

Princess Rosette

You may imagine how astonished the princess was! "Is our vessel doing a dance upon the water?" she exclaimed; "I do not remember ever to have been so uncomfortable as I am to-night." And all the time Frillikin was barking as though he had taken leave of his senses.

The wicked nurse and the boatman heard him from afar. "Do you hear that?" they exclaimed; "it is that funny little dog drinking our very good health with his mistress! Let us make haste and get ashore." By this time, you must understand, they were lying off the capital of the King of the Peacocks.

A hundred carriages had been sent to the water's edge by the king. These were drawn by animals of every kind—lions, bears, stags, wolves, horses, oxen, asses, eagles, and peacocks. The carriage in which Princess Rosette was to be borne was drawn by six blue monkeys which could leap and dance upon the tight-rope and perform endless amusing antics; these had trappings of crimson velvet, studded with gold plates.

Sixty young girls awaited the coming of the princess. They had been selected by the king to be her maids of honour, and their attire, of every colour of the rainbow, shone with ornaments of which gold and silver were the least precious.

The nurse had taken great pains over the toilette of her daughter. She had decked her out in Rosette's most beautiful gown, and placed her diamonds on her head. But nothing could disguise the fact that she was an ugly little fright. Her hair was black and greasy, she was cross-eyed and bow-legged, and in the middle of her back she had a big hump. Moreover she was ill-tempered and sulky, and was for ever grumbling.

When the people of Peacock Land saw her disembark

they were so completely taken aback that none could say a word.

"What's the matter with you all?" she demanded; "have you

She was an ugly little fright

all gone to sleep? Bring me something to eat at once, do you hear? I'll have the lot of you hanged, precious riff-raff that you are!"

"What a horrible creature!" murmured the citizens amongst themselves, when they heard these threats; "as ill-tempered as she is ugly! A nice bride for our king, or I am much mistaken! It was hardly worth the trouble to bring her all the way across the world." The girl meantime continued to behave in most domineering fashion, giving slaps and blows to every one without the slightest provocation.

The procession, being very large, was obliged to move slowly, and as the carriage bore her along she comported herself as though she were a queen. But all the peacocks, who had perched upon the trees to greet her as she passed, and had arranged to call out "Long live the beautiful Queen Rosette!" cried out when they saw how horrible she was: "Fie! fie! how ugly she is!" This enraged her, and she called out to her escort: "Kill those impudent peacocks: they are insulting me!" But the peacocks flew nimbly away, and laughed at her.

The rascally boatman was witness of all that occurred, and whispered to the nurse: "Things are not going well for us, my good woman: your daughter should have been prettier."

"Hold your tongue, stupid!" she replied; "or you will get us into trouble."

Word was brought to the king that the princess was approaching. "Well," said he; "did her brothers speak the truth? Is she more beautiful than her portrait?"

"Sire," said the courtiers, "if she is only as beautiful, that should be enough."

"Very true!" exclaimed the king. "I shall be content with that. Let us go and see her."

He could tell from the din which arose from the courtyard that the princess had arrived, but the only words he could hear plainly amidst the hubbub were cries of "Fie! fie! how ugly she is!" He supposed people must be referring to some dwarf or pet creature which she had perhaps brought with her, for it never entered his head that it could be the princess herself who was meant.

The portrait of Rosette, uncovered, was hoisted on the end of a long pole, and carried in front of the king, who walked in state with his barons and peacocks, and the ambassadors from neighbouring kingdoms in his train. Great was the impatience of the King of the Peacocks to behold his dear Rosette; but when at length he did set eyes on her—gracious heavens, it was a wonder the shock did not kill him on the spot! He flew into a most terrible rage, rending his clothes, and refusing to go near her. Indeed, she frightened him.

"What!" he cried; "have those two dastardly prisoners the impudence to mock me thus, and propose that I should wed such a loathsome creature as that? They shall die for it! Away with that hussy and her nurse, and the fellow who brought them here; cast them into the dungeon of my keep!"

Now the king and his brother, who had heard in prison that their sister was expected, had attired themselves handsomely to receive her. But instead of the prison being opened and their liberty restored, as they had anticipated, there came the gaoler with a squad of soldiers, and made them descend into a black dungeon, swarming with vile creatures, where the water was up to their necks. Never were two people more astounded or more distressed. "Alas!" they cried to each other; "this is a doleful wedding feast for us! What has brought this unhappy fate upon us?" They did not know what in the world to think, except that it was desired to compass their death, and this reflection filled them with melancholy.

Princess Rosette

Three days passed and they heard not a word of anything. At the end of the third day the King of the Peacocks came and hurled insults at them through a hole in the wall.

"You called yourselves King and Prince to trap me," he shouted to them, "and sought thus to make me promise to wed your sister. But you are nought but a couple of beggars, not worth the water you drink. You shall be sent for trial, and the judges will make short work of your case—the rope to hang you with is being plaited already!"

"Not so fast, King of the Peacocks," replied the captive monarch, angrily, "or you will have cause to repent it! I am a king like yourself: I rule over a fair land, I have robes and crowns and treasure in plenty. I pledge my all to the truth of what I say. You must be joking to talk of hanging us—of what have we robbed you?"

The King of the Peacocks hardly knew what to make of this bold and confident challenge. He was almost of a mind to spare their lives and let them take their sister away. But his Chancellor, an arrant flatterer, egged him on, whispering that if he did not avenge himself, he would be the laughing-stock of the whole world, and would be looked upon as a mere twopenny-halfpenny monarch. Thus influenced, he vowed he would not pardon them, and ordered their trial to take place.

This did not take long, for it was only necessary to compare side by side the portrait of the true Princess Rosette with the actual person who had come in her place and claimed identity with her. The prisoners were forthwith condemned to have their heads cut off as a penalty for lying, in that they brought the king an ugly little peasant girl after promising a beautiful princess.

Princess Rosette

The sentence was read with great ceremony at the prison, but the victims protested that they had spoken the truth, that their sister was indeed a princess, and that there was something at the back of all this which they did not understand. They asked for a respite of seven days, that they might have an opportunity of establishing their innocence; and though the King of the Peacock's wrath was such that he had great difficulty in granting this concession, he agreed to it at length.

Something must now be told of what was happening to poor Princess Rosette while all these events were taking place at the Court.

Great was her astonishment, and Frillikin's also, to find herself, when day came, in mid-ocean without boat or any means of assistance. She fell to weeping, and cried so long and bitterly that all the fishes were moved to compassion. She knew not what to do, nor what would become of her.

"There is no doubt," she said, "that I have been thrown into the sea by order of the King of the Peacocks. He has regretted his promise to marry me, and to be rid of me without fuss he has had me drowned. A strange way for a man to behave! And I should have loved him so much, and we should have been so happy together!"

These thoughts made her weep the more, for she could not dispel her fancy for him.

For two days she floated hither and thither over the sea, soaked to the skin, nigh dead with cold, and so nearly benumbed that but for little Frillikin, who snuggled to her bosom, and kept a little warmth in her, she must have perished a hundred times. She was famished with hunger, but on seeing some oysters in their shells

she took and ate as many as would appease her. Frillikin did
the same, but only to keep himself alive, for he did not like
them.

She floated hither and thither

When night fell Rosette was filled with terror. "Bark, Frillikin," she said to her dog; "keep on barking, or the soles will
come and eat us!" So Frillikin barked all night.

When morning came the bed was not far off the shore. Hereabouts there lived, all alone, a kindly old man. His home was a

little hut where no one ever came, and as he had no desire for worldly goods he was very poor. He was astonished when he heard the barking of Frillikin, for no dogs ever came that way; and supposing that some travellers must have missed their road, he

A kindly old man

went out with the good-natured intention of putting them right. Suddenly he saw the princess and Frillikin floating out at sea. The princess caught sight of him, and stretching out her arms to him, cried:

"Save me, kind old man, or I shall perish; two whole days have I been floating thus."

He was filled with pity when he heard her speak thus dolefully, and went to his house to fetch a big crook. He waded out till the water was up to his neck, and after being nearly drowned two or three times he succeeded in grappling the bed and drawing it to the shore.

Princess Rosette

Rosette and Frillikin were delighted to find themselves once more on land. Rosette thanked the good man warmly. She accepted the offer of his cloak, and having wrapped herself in it walked barefoot to his hut. There he lit a little fire of dry straw, and took from a chest his dead wife's best dress, with a pair of stockings and shoes, which the princess put on. Clad thus in peasant's attire, with Frillikin gambolling round her to amuse her, she looked as beautiful as ever.

The old man saw plainly that Rosette was a great lady, for the coverlets of her bed were of gold and silver, and her mattress of satin. He begged her to tell him her story, promising not to repeat a word if she so desired. She related everything from beginning to end—not without tears, for she still believed that the King of the Peacocks had meant her to be drowned.

"What are we to do, my child?" said the old man. "A great lady like you is accustomed to live on dainties, and I have only black bread and radishes—very poor fare for you. But I will go, if you will let me, and tell the King of the Peacocks that you are here. There is not the least doubt he will marry you, once he has seen you."

"He is a bad man," said Rosette; "he wanted me to die. If only you can supply me with a small basket to fasten on my dog's neck, it will be exceedingly bad luck if he does not bring us back something to eat."

The old man handed a basket to the princess, and she hung it round Frillikin's neck with these words: "Find the best stew-pot in the town, and bring me back whatever is inside it." Off went Frillikin to the town, and as he could think of no better stew-pot than the king's, he made his way into the royal kitchen. Having found the stew-pot, he cleverly extricated its contents and returned to the house.

"Now go back to the larder," said Rosette, "and bring the best that you can find there."

Away went Frillikin to the larder and took some white bread, some choice wine, and an assortment of fruit and sweets. In fact, he took as much as he could carry.

When the King of the Peacocks should have dined there was nothing in the stew-pot and nothing in the larder. Everybody gazed blankly at everybody else, and the king flew into a terrible rage. "Oh, very good," said he; "it seems I am to have no dinner! Well, put the spits to the fire, and see to it that some good roast joints are ready for me this evening!"

When evening came the princess said to Frillikin: "Find the best kitchen in the town and bring me a nice roast joint." Off went Frillikin to carry out this order from his mistress. Thinking there could be no better kitchen than the king's, he slipped in quietly when the cooks' backs were turned, and took off the spit a roast joint, which looked so good that the mere sight of it gave one an appetite. His basket was full when he brought it back to the princess, but she sent him off again to the larder, and from there he carried away all the king's sweetmeats and dessert.

The king was exceedingly hungry, having had no dinner, and ordered supper betimes. But there was nothing to eat, and he went to bed in a frightful temper. Next day at dinner and supper it was just the same. For three days the king had nothing to eat or drink, for every time he sat down at table it was found that everything had been stolen.

The Chancellor, being very much afraid that the king would

die, went and hid in a corner of the kitchen, whence he could keep the stew-pot on the fire constantly in view. To his astonishment he saw a little green dog, with only one ear, creep in stealthily, take the lid off the pot, and transfer the meat to his basket. He followed it in order to find out where it went, and saw it leave the town. Still pursuing, he came to the house of the good old man. He went immediately to the king and told him that it was to a poor peasant's house that every morning and evening his dinner and supper vanished.

The king was mightily astonished, and ordered investigations to be made. The Chancellor, to curry favour, volunteered to go himself, and took with him a posse of archers. They found the old man at dinner with the princess, and the pair of them eating the king's provisions. They seized and bound them with strong ropes, not forgetting to deal in like manner with Frillikin.

"To-morrow," said the king, when he was told that the prisoners had arrived, "the seven days' grace expires which I granted to those miscreants who insulted me. They shall go to execution with the stealers of my dinner."

When the King of the Peacocks entered the court of justice the old man flung himself on his knees, and declared that he would narrate all that had happened. As he told his story the king eyed the beautiful princess, and was touched by her weeping. When presently the good man declared that her name was the Princess Rosette, and that she had been thrown into the sea, he bounded three times into the air, despite the weak state in which he was after going so long without food, and ran to embrace her. As he undid the cords which bound her he cried out that he loved her with all his heart.

Princess Rosette

A guard had been sent for the princes, who approached just then. They came sadly with bowed heads, for they believed the hour of their execution had come. The nurse and her daughter were brought in at the same moment. Recognition was instant on

all sides. Rosette flung herself into her brothers' arms, while the nurse and her daughter, with the boatman, fell on their knees and prayed for clemency. So joyous was the occasion that the king and the princess pardoned them. The good old man was handsomely rewarded, and given quarters at the palace for the rest of his life.

Finally, the King of the Peacocks made all amends in his power to the royal brothers, expressing his deep regret at having ill-treated them. The nurse delivered up to Rosette her beautiful dresses and the bushel of golden crowns, and the wedding festivities lasted for fifteen days. Every one was happy, not excepting Frillikin, who ate nothing but partridge wings for the rest of his life.

LITTLE TOM THUMB

ONCE upon a time there lived a wood-cutter and his wife, who had seven children, all boys. The eldest was only ten years old, and the youngest was seven. People were astonished that the wood-cutter had had so many children in so short a time, but the reason was that his wife delighted in children, and never had less than two at a time.

They were very poor, and their seven children were a great tax on them, for none of them was yet able to earn his own living. And they were troubled also because the youngest was very delicate and seldom spoke a word. They mistook for stupidity what was in reality a mark of good sense.

This youngest boy was very little. At his birth he was scarcely bigger than a man's thumb, and he was called in consequence "Little Tom Thumb." The poor child was the scapegoat of the family, and got the blame for everything. All the same, he was the sharpest and shrewdest of the brothers, and if he spoke but little he listened much.

There came a very bad year, when the famine was so great that these poor people resolved to get rid of their family. One evening, after the children had gone to bed, the wood-cutter was sitting in the chimney-corner with his wife. His heart was heavy with sorrow as he said to her:

"It must be plain enough to you that we can no longer feed

our children. I cannot see them starve before my eyes, and I have made up my mind to take them to-morrow to the forest and lose them there. It will be easy enough to manage, for while they are amusing themselves by collecting faggots we have only to disappear without their seeing us."

"Ah!" cried the wood-cutter's wife, "do you mean to say you are capable of letting your own children be lost?"

In vain did her husband remind her of their terrible poverty; she could not agree. She was poor, but she was their mother. In the end, however, reflecting what a grief it would be to see them starve, she consented to the plan and went weeping to bed.

Little Tom Thumb had heard all that was said. Having discovered, when in bed, that serious talk was going on, he had got up softly, and had slipped under his father's stool in order to listen without being seen. He went back to bed, but did not sleep a wink for the rest of the night, thinking over what he had better do. In the morning he rose very early and went to the edge of a brook. There he filled his pockets with little white pebbles and came quickly home again.

They all set out, and little Tom Thumb said not a word to his brothers of what he knew.

They went into a forest which was so dense that when only ten paces apart they could not see each other. The wood-cutter set about his work, and the children began to collect twigs to make faggots. Presently the father and mother, seeing them busy at their task, edged gradually away, and then hurried off in haste along a little narrow footpath.

When the children found they were alone they began to cry and call out with all their might. Little Tom Thumb let them cry, being confident that they would get back home again. For on the way he had dropped the little white stones which he carried in his pocket all along the path.

"Don't be afraid, brothers," he said presently; "our parents have left us here, but I will take you home again. Just follow me."

They fell in behind him, and he led them straight to their house by the same path which they had taken to the forest. At first they dared not go in, but placed themselves against the door, where they could hear everything their father and mother were saying.

Now the wood-cutter and his wife had no sooner reached home than the lord of the manor sent them a sum of ten crowns which had been owing from him for a long time, and of which they had given up hope. This put new life into them, for the poor creatures were extremely hungry.

The wood-cutter sent his wife off to the butcher at once, and as it was such a long time since he had had anything to eat, she bought three times as much as a supper for two required.

When they found themselves once more at table, the wood-cutter's wife began to lament.

"Alas! where are our poor children now?" she said; "they could make a good meal off what we have left. Mind you, William, it was you who wished to lose them: I declared over and over again that we should repent it. What are they doing now in that forest? Merciful heavens, perhaps the wolves have already found them! A monster you must be to lose your children in this way!"

At last the wood-cutter lost patience, for she repeated more than twenty times that he would repent it, and that she had told him so. He threatened to beat her if she did not hold her tongue.

It was not that the wood-cutter was less grieved than his wife, but she browbeat him, and he was of the same opinion as many other people, who like a woman to have the knack of saying the right thing, but not the trick of being always in the right.

"Alas!" cried the wood-cutter's wife, bursting into tears, "where are now my children, my poor children?"

She said it once so loud that the children at the door heard it plainly. Together they all called out:

"Here we are! Here we are!"

She rushed to open the door for them, and exclaimed, as she embraced them:

"How very glad I am to see you again, dear children! You must be very tired and very hungry. And you, Peterkin, how muddy you are—come and let me wash you!"

This Peterkin was her eldest son. She loved him more than all the others because he was inclined to be red-headed, and she herself was rather red.

They sat down at the table and ate with an appetite which it did their parents good to see. They all talked at once, as they recounted the fears they had felt in the forest.

The good souls were delighted to have their children with them again, and the pleasure continued as long as the ten crowns lasted. But when the money was all spent they relapsed into their former sadness. They again resolved to lose the children, and to lead them much further away than they had done the first time, so as to do the job thoroughly. But though they were careful not to speak openly about it, their conversation did not escape little Tom

Little Tom Thumb

Thumb, who made up his mind to get out of the situation as he had done on the former occasion.

But though he got up early to go and collect his little stones, he found the door of the house doubly locked, and he could not carry out his plan.

He could not think what to do until the wood-cutter's wife gave them each a piece of bread for breakfast. Then it occurred to him to use the bread in place of the stones, by throwing crumbs along the path which they took, and he tucked it tight in his pocket.

Their parents led them into the thickest and darkest part of the forest, and as soon as they were there slipped away by a side-path and left them. This did not much trouble little Tom Thumb, for he believed he could easily find the way back by means of the bread which he had scattered wherever he walked. But to his dismay he could not discover a single crumb. The birds had come along and eaten it all.

They were in sore trouble now, for with every step they strayed further, and became more and more entangled in the forest. Night came on and a terrible wind arose, which filled them with dreadful alarm. On every side they seemed to hear nothing but the howling of wolves, and they dared not speak or move.

In addition it began to rain so heavily that they were soaked to the skin. At every step they tripped and fell on the wet ground, getting up again covered with mud, not knowing what to do with their hands.

Little Tom Thumb climbed to the top of a tree, in an endeavour to see something. Looking all about him he espied, far away on the other side of the forest, a little light like that of a candle.

Little Tom Thumb

He got down from the tree, and was terribly disappointed to find that when he was on the ground he could see nothing at all.

After they had walked some distance in the direction of the light, however, he caught a glimpse of it again as they were nearing the edge of the forest. At last they reached the house where the light was burning, but not without much anxiety, for every time they had to go down into a hollow they lost sight of it.

They knocked at the door, and a good dame opened to them. She asked them what they wanted.

Little Tom Thumb explained that they were poor children who had lost their way in the forest, and begged her, for pity's sake, to give them a night's lodging.

Noticing what bonny children they all were, the woman began to cry.

"Alas, my poor little dears!" she said: "you do not know the place you have come to! Have you not heard that this is the house of the ogre who owns this forest?"

"Alas, madame!" answered little Tom Thumb, trembling like all the rest of his brothers, "what shall we do? One thing is very certain: if you do not take us in, the wolves of the forest will find us this very night. Perhaps your husband may take pity on us, if you will plead for us."

The ogre's wife, thinking she might be able to hide them from her husband till the next morning, allowed them to come in, and put them to warm near a huge fire, where a whole sheep was cooking on the spit for the ogre's supper.

Just as they were beginning to get warm they heard two or three great bangs at the door. The ogre had returned. His wife hid them quickly under the bed and ran to open the door.

A good dame opened the door

Little Tom Thumb

The first thing the ogre did was to ask whether supper was ready and the wine opened. Blood was still dripping from the sheep, but it seemed all the better to him for that. He sniffed to right and left, declaring that he could smell fresh meat.

"Indeed!" said his wife. "It must be the calf which I have just dressed that you smell."

"*I smell fresh meat,* I tell you," shouted the ogre, eyeing his wife askance; "and there is something going on here which I do not understand."

With these words he got up from the table and went straight to the bed.

"Aha!" said he; "so this is the way you deceive me, wicked woman that you are! It's lucky for you that you are old and tough! I am expecting three ogre friends of mine to pay me a visit in the next few days, and here is a treat for them!"

One after another he dragged the children out from under the bed.

The poor things threw themselves on their knees, imploring mercy; but they had to deal with the most cruel of all ogres. Off he went to get his magic staff and a large knife, which he sharpened, as he drew near the poor children, on a long stone in his left hand.

He had already seized one of them when his wife called out to him. "What do you want to change them now for?" she said; "will it not be time enough to-morrow?"

"Hold your tongue," replied the ogre in an ugly tone of voice.

"But you have such a lot of meat," rejoined his wife; "look, there are a calf, two sheep, and half a pig."

Little Tom Thumb

"You are right," said the ogre; "give them a good supper to fatten them up, and take them to bed."

The good woman was overjoyed and brought them a splendid supper; but the poor little wretches were so cowed with fright that they could not eat.

As for the ogre, he went back to his drinking, very pleased to have such good entertainment for his friends. He drank a dozen cups more than usual, and was obliged to go off to bed early, for the wine had gone somewhat to his head.

Now the ogre had seven daughters who as yet were only children. These little ogresses all had the most lovely complexions, but they also had little round grey eyes, crooked noses, and very large mouths, with long and exceeding sharp teeth, set far apart. They were not so very wicked at present, but they showed great promise, for already they were in the habit of catching little animals and sucking their blood.

They had gone to bed early, and were all seven in a great bed, each with a frilly white nightcap upon her head.

In the same room there was another bed, equally large. In this the ogre's wife put the seven little boys, and then went to sleep herself beside her husband.

Little Tom Thumb was fearful lest the ogre should suddenly regret that he had not enchanted himself and his brothers the evening before. Having noticed that the ogre's daughters all had frilly white nightcaps upon their heads, he got up in the middle of the night and softly placed his own cap and those of his brothers' on their heads. Before doing so, he carefully removed the nightcaps, putting them on his own and his brothers' heads. In this way, if the ogre were to feel like

He could smell fresh meat

enchanting them that night he would mistake the girls for the boys, and *vice versa.*

Things fell out just as he had anticipated. The ogre, waking up at midnight, regretted that he had postponed till the morrow what he could have done overnight. Jumping briskly out of bed, he seized his magic staff and his knife, crying: "Now then, let's see how the little rascals are; we won't make the same mistake twice!"

He groped his way up to his daughters' room, and approached the bed in which were the seven little boys. All were sleeping, with the exception of little Tom Thumb, who was numb with fear when he felt the ogre's hand, as it touched the head of each brother in turn, reach his own.

"Upon my word," said the ogre, as he felt the frilly nightcaps; "a nice job I was going to make of it! It is very evident that I drank a little too much last night!"

Forthwith he went to the bed where his daughters were, and here he felt the little boys' caps.

"Aha, here are the little scamps!" he cried; "now for a smart bit of work!"

With these words, and without a moment's hesitation, he transformed his seven daughters into sheep and cut their throats. Then, well satisfied with his work, he went back to bed beside his wife.

No sooner did little Tom Thumb hear him snoring than he woke up his brothers, bidding them dress quickly and follow him. They crept quietly down to the garden, and jumped from the wall. All through the night they ran in haste and terror, without the least idea of where they were going.

When the ogre woke up he said to his wife:

Little Tom Thumb

"Go upstairs and dress those little rascals who were here last night."

The ogre's wife was astonished at her husband's kindness, never doubting that he meant her to go and put on their clothes. She went upstairs, and was horrified to discover her seven daughters changed into sheep, with their throats cut.

She fell at once into a swoon, which is the way of most women in similar circumstances.

The ogre, thinking his wife was very long in carrying out his orders, went up to help her, and was no less astounded than his wife at the terrible spectacle which confronted him.

"What's this I have done?" he exclaimed. "I will be revenged on the wretches, and quickly, too!"

He threw a jugful of water over his wife's face, and having brought her round ordered her to fetch his seven-league boots, so that he might overtake the children.

He set off over the countryside, and strode far and wide until he came to the road along which the poor children were travelling. They were not more than a few yards from their home when they saw the ogre striding from hill-top to hill-top, and stepping over rivers as though they were merely tiny streams.

Little Tom Thumb espied near at hand a cave in some rocks. In this he hid his brothers, and himself followed them in, while continuing to keep a watchful eye upon the movements of the ogre.

Now the ogre was feeling very tired after so much fruitless marching (for seven-league boots are very fatiguing to their wearer), and felt like taking a little rest. As it happened, he went and sat down on the very rock beneath which the little boys were

He set off over the countryside

hiding. Overcome with weariness, he had not sat there long before he fell asleep and began to snore terribly.

Little Tom Thumb told his brothers to flee at once to their home while the ogre was still sleeping soundly, and not to worry about him. They took his advice and ran quickly home.

Little Tom Thumb now approached the ogre and gently pulled off his boots, which he at once donned himself. The boots were very heavy and very large, but being enchanted boots they had the faculty of growing larger or smaller according to the leg they had to suit. Consequently they always fitted as though they had been made for the wearer.

He went straight to the ogre's house, where he found the ogre's wife weeping over the seven dead sheep.

"Your husband," said little Tom Thumb, "is in great danger, for he has been captured by a gang of thieves, and the latter have sworn to kill him if he does not hand over all his gold and silver. Just as they had the dagger at his throat, he caught sight of me and begged me to come to you and thus rescue him from his terrible plight. You are to give me everything of value which he possesses, without keeping back a thing, otherwise he will be slain without mercy. As the matter is urgent he wished me to wear his seven-league boots, to save time, and also to prove to you that I am no impostor."

The ogre's wife, in great alarm, gave him immediately all that she had.

Little Tom Thumb, laden with all the ogre's wealth, forthwith repaired to his father's house, where he was received with great joy.

Little Tom Thumb

Many people do not agree about this last adventure, and pretend that little Tom Thumb never committed this theft from the ogre, and only took the seven-league boots, about which he had no compunction, since they were only used by the ogre for catching his victims. These folks assert that they are in a position to know, having been guests at the wood-cutter's cottage. They further say that when little Tom Thumb had put on the ogre's boots, he went off to the Court, where he knew there was great anxiety concerning the result of a battle which was being fought by an army two hundred leagues away.

They say that he went to the king and undertook, if desired, to bring news of the army before the day was out; and that the king promised him a large sum of money if he could carry out his project.

Little Tom Thumb brought news that very night, and this first errand having brought him into notice, he made as much money as he wished. For not only did the king pay him handsomely to carry orders to the army, but many ladies at the court gave him anything he asked to get them news of their lovers, and this was his greatest source of income. He was occasionally entrusted by wives with letters to their husbands, but they paid him so badly, and this branch of the business brought him in so little, that he did not even bother to reckon what he made from it.

After acting as courier for some time, and amassing great wealth thereby, little Tom Thumb returned to his father's house, and was there greeted with the greatest joy imaginable. He made all his family comfortable, buying newly-created positions for his father and brothers. In this way he set them all up, not forgetting at the same time to look well after himself.

Laden with all the ogre's wealth

THE YELLOW DWARF

THERE once was a queen who had only one daughter, and finding herself a widow, she was so afraid of losing her only child that she never corrected any of her faults. Because of this, Princess Toutebelle, as she was called, became so proud and vain that she despised everybody. Yet she was so beautiful that twenty kings vied with each other to please her, and not a day passed that she did not receive seven or eight thousand sonnets, and as many odes, madrigals, and songs, which were sent by all the poets in the universe. Nobody ventured to pretend to the honor of being her husband, though everybody desired it, for how was it possible to touch a heart of that description? Her lovers complained bitterly of her cruelty, and her mother, who very much wished her to be married, saw no means of persuading her to choose a husband.

When the queen had exhausted all possible conversations with her daughter on the subject of marriage, she bitterly regretted her earlier indulgences. And, in despair, she sought the advice of the celebrated Fairy of the Desert. It was not easy to see the Fairy, for she was guarded by fierce lions, to whom it was necessary to throw a special cake made of millet-seed, sugar-candy, and crocodiles' eggs. The queen herself prepared the cake, and putting it into a little hand-basket, she set out on her journey. After a while, tired with walking so far, she lay down at the foot of a tree to take a

201

rest. Naturally, she fell asleep, but on re-awakening she found her basket empty and the cake gone. To complete her misfortune, she heard the lions coming, roaring tremendously.

"Alas! What will become of me?" she exclaimed. "I shall be devoured." She wept, and clung to the tree under which she had slept. At that moment she heard, "Hist! Hist! A-hem! A-hem!" She looked all about her, and raising her eyes, she saw up in the tree a little man not more than a cubit in height. He was eating oranges, and said to her, "Oh! I know you well, queen, and I know how frightened you are that the lions will devour you; and not without reason are you alarmed, for they have devoured many others before you."

"Alas," said the queen, "I should die with less pain if only my dear daughter were married!"

"Ho! You have a daughter?" exclaimed the Yellow Dwarf (for he was the little man in the tree). "Truly I am delighted to hear it, for I have sought a wife by land and sea, and if you promise her to me, I will save you."

The queen looked at him, and was scarcely less frightened at his horrible appearance than the thought of the lions. But at that moment she saw on a nearby hill the lions running towards her. Each had two heads, eight feet, four rows of teeth, and skin as hard as shell and as red as morocco. At this fearsome sight she trembled like a dove, and cried out "My Lord Dwarf, Toutebelle is yours."

A door in the trunk of the orange tree immediately opened, and the queen rushed into it, dropping insensible to the ground. While in this state she was transported to the palace, and placed in her own bed, wherein she awoke and recollected what had befallen her. In the excess of her anxiety she fell into a melancholy so extraordinary that she could scarcely speak, eat, or sleep.

Now Toutebelle, who loved her mother with all her heart, implored her to say what was the matter, but meeting only with excuses and silences, determined that she would seek the advice of the famous Fairy of the Desert, and also consult with her on the question of marrying or remaining single. She took care to knead the cake herself which had the power to appease the lions, and pretending to go to bed early one evening, she went out by a little back staircase, and took the road to the grotto in which the Fairy lived.

Arriving at the orange tree, she found it so covered with fruit that she was seized with an irresistible desire to gather some. She set her basket upon the ground, and plucked some oranges, which she ate. And when she looked again for her basket and cake these had disappeared. She had begun to weep in despair when a frightful little dwarf appeared beside her.

"What are you weeping for?" he said.

"Alas!" replied she, "I have lost my basket and my cake, with which I was to reach the abode of the Fairy of the Desert."

"Ah!" said the Dwarf, "I am her kinsman, and at least as clever as she is in the matter of giving advice."

"The queen, my mother," replied the princess, "has lately become so despondent that I fear for her life. I fancy that I am, perhaps, the cause of it; for she wishes me to marry, and I confess to you that I have not yet seen any one I think worthy of me. It is for this reason that I would consult the Fairy."

"Do not trouble yourself," said the Yellow Dwarf, "I am

better fitted than she to enlighten you on such subjects. The queen, your mother, has promised you to me in marriage!"

"Oh! You must be mistaken," cried the princess, recoiling some paces. "Surely she would have told me, and I am too much interested in the matter for her to engage me without my previous consent." At that moment the poor princess heard the roars of approaching lions. Frightened nearly to death, she cried out: "Save me! Save me! I would rather marry all the dwarfs in the universe than perish in so frightful a manner."

Whereupon she fell into a deep swoon, from which she awoke in her own bed. The only sign of her terrible adventure was a little ring made of a single red hair on her finger, which fitted so closely that the skin might have been taken off sooner than the ring.

Toutebelle saw no better way of getting out of her dilemma than by marrying a great king with whom the Yellow Dwarf would not dare to dispute so glorious a prize. And so, at length and after much thought, she consented to marry the king of the gold mines, a very powerful and handsome man, who had loved her passionately for several years without any hope that his affection would be returned. The obvious importance of becoming acquainted with her future husband induced the princess to study him carefully, and she discovered in him so much merit, so much sense, such deep and delicate feeling—in short, so fine a mind in so perfect a body, that she began to return his affection.

At last the day of the wedding arrived. Trumpets announced throughout the city the commencement of the ceremony, and the streets were carpeted and strewn with flowers. Toutebelle was all diamonds down to her very shoes; a magnificent crown adorned her head, and her hair fell in curls to her feet. The king of the gold mines was no less perfect in his appearance, and the happy couple were advancing to the altar, when they saw the Yellow Dwarf entering the long gallery in a carriage drawn by two large turkey-cocks.

He took three turns around the gallery before he spoke a word, then stopping in the center of it, he cried in a threatening manner:

"Ho! Do you fancy you can break your promise to the Yellow Dwarf? But for me the lions would have devoured you! Consider what you are about to do, for I swear that if you do not marry me you will die."

The king of the gold mines, enraged at this opposition to his marriage, advanced upon the Dwarf with sword in hand. Where-upon he drew a large cutlass, and challenging the king to single combat, descended into the courtyard of the palace amidst an extraordinary uproar. Scarcely had they confronted each other, than the sun became suddenly as red as blood, and it grew so dark that they could hardly see. It thundered and lightened as if it was the end of the world, and the two turkey-cocks appeared at the side of the Yellow Dwarf like giants, taller than mountains, casting out flames from their mouths and eyes. All these horrors did not shake the courage of the young king, and he had just dealt the Yellow Dwarf a mortal wound when the Fairy of the Desert appeared. Her head was covered with long serpents, and mounted upon a winged griffin and armed with a lance, she struck the king himself with a deadly blow. Then, with the serpents hissing loudly, she disappeared into thin air. The princess uttered a terrible shriek, and unable to survive her lover, fell upon his body and her spirit quickly fled to join his.

The Yellow Dwarf

Princess Toutebelle and the king of the gold mines were buried together side by side, and from their graves grew two beautiful palm trees. Still cherishing a faithful love for each other, they joined their branches in fond embrace, and so immortalized their passion.

THE END